A Death in Chelsea

A Death in Chelsea

A Lady in Blue Mystery Novel

H L Marsay

TULE
PUBLISHING

A Death in Chelsea
Copyright© 2024 H L Marsay
Tule Publishing First Printing February 2024

The Tule Publishing, Inc.

ALL RIGHTS RESERVED

First Publication by Tule Publishing 2024

Cover design by Patrick Knowles

No part of this book may be used or reproduced in any manner
whatsoever without written permission except in the case of brief
quotations embodied in critical articles and reviews.

This is a work of fiction. Names, characters, places, and incidents are
products of the author's imagination or are used fictitiously. Any
resemblance to actual events, locales, organizations, or persons, living or
dead, is entirely coincidental.

AI was not used to create any part of this book and no part of this book
may be used for generative training.

ISBN: 978-1-961544-87-1

Dedication

In memory of Edith Smith,
the United Kingdom's first policewoman.

Chapter One

"DOROTHY! YOU MUST come quickly. I've found a dead body." Dorothy Peto rubbed her eyes and wondered if it was possible she was still dreaming. The ringing of the telephone had woken her, and she'd stumbled out of bed and down the hallway to answer it. The longcase clock standing next to her told her it was just after six.

"Margaret, is that you?" she asked, stifling a yawn and jamming a finger in her ear so she could hear the voice at the end of the crackling line more clearly.

"Yes, please come quickly. It's poor Mr Gaskill. He's dead."

"Who?" asked Dorothy but Margaret had already hung up.

DOROTHY WAITED FOR the omnibus to come to a juddering halt, then stepped off on to Glebe Place with some relief. Although it was still early and a Sunday, the journey from Bloomsbury to Chelsea had been awfully hot and crowded. A taxi would have been quicker and more pleasant, but they were almost impossible to find these days. So many motor cabs had been converted into ambulances and almost all the horses had been taken for the army.

She hurried down the road and round the corner on to Cheyne Row. She checked her watch. Margaret had telephoned her almost an hour ago. She'd sounded terribly agitated. After her call, Dorothy had dressed immediately and dashed across the city.

Margaret Damer Dawson was commandant of the Women Police Volunteers, the group that she had set up with Dorothy, Mary Allen and Nina Boyle to help the regular police when war broke out. Normally, Margaret would have had Mary with her, but both she and Nina were away helping train new recruits. Over the last twelve months, the number of WPV members had grown rapidly and the women, patrolling in their dark blue uniforms, had become a familiar sight on the country's streets. This morning, nobody gave Dorothy a second glance as she walked briskly towards Margaret's house.

As she approached the row of smart terraced town houses, she saw Margaret hurrying towards her, accompanied as always by her three dogs: Topsy and Skip, the two spaniels, and Herbert, the basset hound.

"Oh, Dorothy, thank heavens you are here," she gasped breathlessly.

"Margaret, are you all right? It sounded like you were saying someone had died."

"They have! Poor Mr Gaskill. I woke early. It was so hot last night, and I never sleep well when Mary is away. So I went to open my bedroom curtains and there he was!"

"In your bedroom?"

"No, Dorothy! Of course not. In his garden. He lives next door." She gestured to twelve Cheyne Row. It was identical to her own house, number ten. Four elegant storeys high with a basement and built of brick with black wrought-iron railings. The front door of number twelve was wide open.

"Come and take a look for yourself," Margaret called over her shoulder as she made her way inside. Dorothy followed her through the door. The layout of the house's interior was also the same as Margaret's, but the décor was far more old-fashioned and a little shabby. The phrase 'faded grandeur' came to mind.

"Did Mr Gaskill live alone?" she enquired.

"Yes," replied Margaret, "well, except for the servants. There's a butler, a cook and a maid."

They stepped out into the garden and Dorothy saw at once poor Mr Gaskill. Wearing a faded tartan dressing gown with dark pinstriped trousers beneath, he was sprawled out across the neatly trimmed lawn next to a beautifully carved stone bird table. As she got closer, she could see he was a thin, frail-looking man, who she guessed must be in his seventies. She knelt down to check for a pulse, but as soon as she touched his papery skin, she knew he was dead. Despite the heat of the early morning sun, he was stone cold. Running across his forehead was a dried trickle of blood. His still-clenched fist was full of birdseed.

"He must have come out to feed the birds," she said.

"Yes, he does so every morning," explained Margaret. "At seven o'clock precisely. Mary and I always joke that we could set our watches by him, but when I opened the curtains, it was half past five. I was quite stunned to see him outside already. At first, I thought the heat must have affected him too and he was simply resting. Well, you know how poor my eyesight is, Dorothy. Then I put my spectacles on and that's when I saw him properly. I opened the window and called his name, but there was no response so I dashed over here."

"Where were the servants?"

"They were just getting up. They thought he was still in bed. Mrs Platt the cook and Connie the maid were awfully upset. I told Duckworth the butler to take them down into the kitchen."

"Have you telephoned the police?" asked Dorothy.

"Yes. I only spoke to a desk sergeant. The silly man asked me if I was sure I hadn't been dreaming. Such a cheek! Anyway, I left my details and he promised to pass them on and I told Annie to try telephoning again."

Dorothy nodded although she wasn't convinced Margaret's maid was the best person to enlist for such an important task. The young woman always leapt out of her skin whenever the telephone rang.

She stood up and looked around the garden. Like the house, it was almost identical to Margaret's. It was walled on all sides with a small wooden door leading out on to Cheyne Walk, which ran along the river. There were two flower beds planted with roses on either side of the lawn and as well as the bird table, there was an equally ornate birdbath at the other end of the garden.

"Do you think he might have fallen and hit his head on the bird table?" asked Margaret. "The leather on the sole of his slipper is coming away. He could have tripped."

Dorothy bent down. It was true. Like his dressing gown, the dead man's slippers were old and worn, but she shook her head.

"I don't think so. There isn't any blood on the stone base of the bird table," she said.

Margaret's hand flew to her mouth. "Oh my goodness," she gasped. "Then you think someone may have attacked him. How dreadful! In his own garden. And this is such a nice, quiet neighbourhood. Who could have done such a thing?"

"A burglar perhaps? They could have come through that door at the bottom of the garden. I wonder if it's locked."

Dorothy was about to go and check, when in the distance, she could hear the unmistakable ringing bell of an approaching police car. "It sounds like Scotland Yard got your message after all. I'll go and tell the servants to prepare themselves to be interviewed. You stay here with the body and, Margaret, do keep the dogs away," she said, pointing to Herbert, who was trying to eat the birdseed out of the dead man's hand.

She quickly made her way back inside the house and down the stairs that led to the kitchen. Sitting around a well-scrubbed pine-topped table were the three servants. A man of about sixty with greying hair and a ruddy complexion, a plump woman of a similar age and a young woman with her dark hair tied in a bun, who was sobbing into her apron. They all rose to their feet when Dorothy opened the door.

"Hello," she said. "My name is Miss Dorothy Peto. Do please sit down. I am a friend of Miss Damer Dawson. I'm so sorry about Mr Gaskill, but I wanted to let you know the police will be arriving shortly. They will probably want to speak to each of you."

The young woman's face turned as white as alabaster. She gripped hold of the table and looked like she might faint at any second.

"The police!" she cried. "Why do I have to talk to them? I won't be able to tell them anything."

"Calm down, Connie," ordered the man. He nodded to Dorothy. "I'm Duckworth, the butler, miss. This is Mrs Platt, the cook, and Connie Beal, the parlour maid. It's good of you to come and tell us about the police. As you can see, we are all very upset about poor Mr Gaskill."

Connie began sobbing again. Dorothy placed a hand on her shoulder.

"Don't worry. They will only want to know if you saw anything that might help them. If you would like me to, I'll sit with you while you are questioned," she offered. Before war had broken out, she and Nina had been campaigning for women and children to be treated more fairly by the justice system, including being allowed to have another woman present when they were being interviewed. "Please sit down," she repeated. "Let me make you all some tea."

Only Connie sank back down into chair. Duckworth and Mrs Platt exchanged a concerned look as Dorothy picked up the kettle that was bubbling on the stove.

"You don't have to do that, miss," said Mrs Platt. "It doesn't seem right."

Dorothy turned and smiled at her as she reached for some cups from the dresser.

"Not at all. I'm happy to," she replied.

The cook smiled back and bustled through into the pantry. "Then I'll fetch us some cake, miss."

"I can do that," Dorothy called after her.

"You are wasting your time, Miss Peto," said Duckworth, straightening his tie. He pointed to his ear. "She's as deaf as a post. No tea for me thank you, miss. I think I'll step outside for a breath of fresh air before the police officers arrive."

He walked a little unsteadily out of the kitchen, leaving the three women together. Dorothy made the tea, while Mrs Platt cut three thick slices of madeira cake and Connie eventually stopped crying.

"How long have you worked for Mr Gaskill?" asked Dorothy as she settled into the chair opposite the cook.

"Nearly twenty years, miss. Mr Duckworth is the same and Connie here has been with us for just over a year now."

"What sort of an employer was he?"

Dorothy saw Mrs Platt catch Connie's eye before she replied.

"Fair but firm I'd say, miss. That's the best way to describe the master. Fair but firm."

Dorothy glanced over at Connie who nodded in agreement, her eyes cast down.

"His death must be a terrible shock for you," continued Dorothy.

"Oh it was," replied the cook. "I thought the master was still in bed. He usually rises at half past six. He gets dressed then comes down to the library. Then he goes to feed the birds so he can watch them while he has his breakfast. I'd come down to the kitchen at my usual time and was about to start making the tea and boiling his eggs—he always started the day with two boiled eggs—when Miss Damer Dawson started hammering on the front door and shouting." She paused and took a sip of her tea. "The next thing I know, Mr Duckworth is down here telling me that the master is dead in the garden."

"Where were you, Connie?" asked Dorothy, as the maid finally seemed to have calmed down.

"I was in the library, miss, tiding up and emptying the grate before the master came down. Except of course he didn't come down." She paused to dry her eyes on the edge of her apron. "I heard Miss Damer Dawson come to the door and I opened the curtains in the library just as she and Mr Duckworth went into the garden. That's when I saw poor Mr Gaskill lying there on the grass."

Mrs Platt reached over and patted her hand, but Dorothy frowned.

"Did Mr Gaskill always have the fire lit in the library? It's been awfully hot all week."

"No, miss," agreed Connie. "It hadn't been lit for over ten days, but he rang the bell yesterday for me to go and light it. It was just after Mr Duckworth had taken him the second post."

"Did he say why? Was he ill? Did he have a chill?"

"No, miss. I don't think so but…" she looked quickly at Mrs Platt "…he seemed a bit out of sorts all day yesterday. All he said was 'light the fire please, Connie'."

"I see, and when was the last time you both saw Mr Gaskill alive?" asked Dorothy. As she was talking to the two female servants, she realised that Duckworth, the butler, was correct. Mrs Platt was taking part in the conversation quite easily, but her eyes were always on the lips of whomever was speaking. Before she answered now, she exchanged another quick look with Connie.

"It was late morning, miss. I'd gone up to discuss the evening's menu with him."

"Did he dine alone last night?"

"No, miss. Mr Gerald Gaskill was here. He's the master's nephew. They usually dined together on a Saturday evening," Mrs Platt explained, then gave Connie a nod of encouragement.

The maid gave a small cough before she spoke. "I last saw the master just after supper, yesterday evening, miss," she said, her eyes fixed on the hem of her apron as she fiddled with it. "I was beginning to clear the table in the dining room as the master and Mr Gerald were going through into the library. I offered to go and close the curtains in there for them as it had grown dark, but Mr Gerald said not to worry and that he would do it. Then I returned to the kitchen, helped with washing the dishes and went up to bed the same time as Mrs Platt. Our bedrooms are in the attic."

"So you both passed the library on your way to bed?"

"No, miss. We used the back staircase not the main one."

"Did Mr Duckworth retire at the same time as you?" asked Dorothy, topping up the cook's cup. Connie's tea and cake remained untouched.

"No, he would be waiting for Mr Gerald to leave. He was in his pantry across the way there. I wished him good-night, but I didn't hear him come upstairs," explained Mrs

Platt pointing through the open door to another closed door opposite the kitchen.

"Did Mr Gaskill have any other visitors yesterday?" enquired Dorothy.

"Yes. Mr Pearson. He's Mr Gaskill's solicitor. Mr Gaskill sent for him. He arrived at three o'clock—I made a tray of tea for Mr Duckworth to take up—and he left at around five o'clock," said Mrs Platt.

"I don't suppose you know why his solicitor was visiting Mr Gaskill?" Dorothy had addressed her question to Connie, but it was Mrs Platt who answered, shaking her head with a smile.

"No, miss. It wasn't our place to know the master's business."

Dorothy nodded although privately she thought the servants almost always knew exactly what was going on. Upstairs, she could hear the sound of heavy footsteps. The police had clearly arrived. She should really go and speak with them.

"I see. Well, thank you for the cake, Mrs Platt. I should be going now, but I promise I'll be here if you need me when the police interview you."

Both women murmured their thanks, as Dorothy rose to her feet and left the kitchen. When she returned upstairs, there was no sign of Duckworth but she found a uniformed policeman now standing guard by the still-open front door and several more out in the garden. Standing next to Margaret and looking down at the body was a tall man in a navy suit, leaning on a walking stick. He turned at the sound of her footsteps and raised his hat.

"Good morning, Miss Peto. I was wondering when I might see you," he said. It was Inspector Derwent of Scotland Yard. Dorothy had met him before, when he'd been investigating the death of two actresses. The scar across his face and his stern demeanour made him seem rather forbidding, but Dorothy had grown used to his ways.

"Oh, Dorothy, there you are," exclaimed Margaret. "I was just explaining to Inspector Derwent that I telephoned you after I called Scotland Yard."

"Yet, you managed to beat us here, Miss Peto."

"Well, it was obvious from Margaret's call that this was a matter of urgency, but it seems the officer Margaret first spoke with was disinclined to believe her story, so perhaps that caused your delay," suggested Dorothy sweetly. "We wondered at first if he could have fallen and hit his head on the bird table, but there's no blood on the base."

"No," replied the inspector, shaking his head, "and unless I'm very much mistaken, he has been dead for several hours. We'll know more when Willerby and Dr Stirk arrive. I take it he wasn't in the habit of wandering around his garden in the early hours of the morning?"

"No," replied Margaret. "As I said, he usually doesn't come out until exactly seven o'clock."

"Have you known the deceased long, Miss Damer Dawson?" asked the inspector.

"We've been neighbours for almost ten years—that's when I moved here—but I wouldn't say I knew him, Inspector. He was a bit of a recluse. Occasionally, we would meet on the street when I was walking the dogs. He was a great animal lover too. No matter the weather, he would always put seed out for the birds."

The inspector didn't look particularly impressed by this piece of information. He knelt down next to the body and carefully raised the left sleeve of the dressing gown.

"Can you recall if he wore a wristwatch, Miss Damer Dawson?" he asked. Dorothy peered down.

"He isn't wearing one now," she commented.

"No," agreed the inspector, "and I would have expected a man of routine to have one."

Margaret's face was creased in concentration. "Let me think now. No, he had one of those old-fashioned fob watches on a chain. It was a gold one. He always used to check it just before he returned to the house. I remember my father had a similar one. He kept it in his dressing gown pocket. Mr Gaskill that is, not my father," she explained.

Inspector Derwent felt in first one of Mr Gaskill's pockets and then the other. "It's not there now," he declared as he stood up straight again.

"If he was attacked, could theft of the watch be the motive?" asked Dorothy.

Before the inspector could reply, one of the uniformed officers, who was near the birdbath shouted out, "Sir! I think we've found something."

Skip and Topsy, Margaret's two spaniels, immediately charged through the flower bed towards the constable.

"Miss Damer Dawson, you have been extremely helpful but could I please ask you to remove your dogs from the garden?" asked the inspector as he made his way towards the birdbath.

"I'm so sorry, Inspector Derwent. They don't mean to

get in the way. They only want to help too, you understand," insisted Margaret.

"I'm sure that is true, Miss Damer Dawson, but the ground is bone dry. My men will find it difficult enough to look for footprints without their assistance," replied the inspector grimly.

"Margaret, why don't we take them down to the river. They must have missed their morning walk in all the excitement," suggested Dorothy. She would have loved to stay at the scene and see what the constable had found, but the expression on Inspector Derwent's face and the way his fingers were drumming against his bad leg told her his patience was due to run out very soon. With a sigh, Margaret reluctantly agreed.

Chapter Two

"IT'S SUCH A shame Inspector Derwent didn't want our help. Herbert has an excellent sense of smell. If there was an intruder in the garden, then I'm sure he would have been able to pick up the villain's scent and track him down," insisted Margaret as they made their way down to the embankment, the three dogs running on ahead scattering pigeons in every direction.

"Has Mr Gaskill always lived alone?" asked Dorothy, keen to move the conversation on from Herbert's nose.

Margaret shook her head and smiled. "No, his grandson Paul used to live with him. He's now a lieutenant in the Royal Berkshire Regiment, I believe. Such a lovely young man and so patriotic. He enlisted as soon as war was declared. His parents both died when they were out in India, and he was only a boy. His father was Mr Gaskill's only son and Paul is his only grandchild."

"Mrs Platt, the cook, mentioned a nephew named Gerald."

The face Margaret made when she heard his name told Dorothy her friend didn't think as highly of Gerald as she did Paul.

"Yes, that's right," she replied. "Oh and there is Emily,

although she isn't really a relative. She was Mr Gaskill's ward, the daughter of a business associate of his. I forget her exact circumstances. She used to live with Hector and Paul, but she's married to Gerald now. Their wedding was last year, about the same time as Paul's twenty-first birthday, not that there was much of a celebration for either. As you could probably see yourself from the house, Mr Gaskill didn't believe in extravagance of any kind." She dabbed at her nose with a handkerchief. "Still he never forgot to feed the birds. I shall rather miss him."

They had reached the river now. Margaret's three dogs were barking at another dog standing on top of one of the barges moored there. The black shaggy-haired creature began snapping and snarling in response. Margaret immediately gave a sharp whistle, and Skip, Topsy and Herbert all came bounding back.

"Would you like to join me for breakfast, Dorothy?" asked Margaret as they returned to Cheyne Row.

"No thank you, Margaret. I don't have much of an appetite."

"Really? Gosh, I'm absolutely famished. Come along, boys. I think we've all earned kippers this morning."

Dorothy waved Margaret goodbye as she and the dogs disappeared through the front door, then she hurried back to number twelve, relieved that the constable on the door didn't stop her entering. She made her way to the door that led from the hall into the garden where she found the inspector and another thin, grey-haired figure bent over the body of Hector Gaskill. Dorothy groaned to herself. It was Dr Wilfrid Stirk, a pathologist who had come out of retirement when war was declared and one of the most obnoxious men Dorothy had ever met.

"Well, Derwent, I can tell you it's definitely murder," she heard him declare confidently as he briefly removed the pipe that seemed to be almost constantly clamped in his mouth. "They wanted to make it look like he'd fallen and hit his head, but the stone base here is square and whatever he was hit with had a rounded edge. Look, it's a curved indentation. It must have been quite a hefty blow too. Cracked his skull I'd say. Death would have been almost instantaneous. But I don't believe he was killed here. He was moved here when he was already dead."

"I thought that might be the case when I saw there was no blood on the grass beneath him. I've got Willerby in the house trying to find out where he was killed. Any thoughts on the time of death, Doctor Stirk?" asked Inspector Derwent.

"Hard to say in this Indian summer but probably between ten o'clock last night and four o'clock this morning. I may know more when I've looked at the contents of his stomach. Find out from the servants at what time he dined last night, will you, Derwent?"

"Certainly. I'm speaking to them next," replied the inspector. Dorothy stepped forward when she heard this and both men turned around. "Did you forget something, Miss Peto?" asked the inspector.

"No, not exactly, but you see, Connie, the maid, was very upset and Mrs Platt, the cook is quite hard of hearing, so I did promise that I would be with them during their interviews."

"Did you now?" said the inspector.

"If you have no objection of course."

Before the inspector could reply there was a loud snort from the doctor as he straightened up.

"What about the butler? Did you promise to hold his hand too? Utter nonsense to have a woman interfering like this. I don't know why you put up with it, Derwent. Well, I'm done here. I'll send word when I've opened him up. Good day."

The doctor strode past Dorothy grumbling to himself while the inspector instructed his men to cover the body. He glanced over in her direction.

"Perhaps you would be good enough to wait inside, Miss Peto, while I arrange to have the body moved to the morgue."

Silently, Dorothy did as he asked, hoping that it was a good sign that he hadn't ordered her to leave the house too. The two of them had worked together after she'd found the body of an actress during a Zeppelin air raid. Being part of that investigation had been the most thrilling thing that had ever happened to her, and the inspector had admitted, a little reluctantly, that she'd been helpful. She'd hoped that meant he would allow her to help with this investigation too, but he was an awfully difficult man to read. Two stretcher-bearers appeared in the hallway. Dorothy didn't want to get in their way, so she stepped through into the library.

"Good morning, Miss Peto! It's jolly nice to see you! I didn't know you would be here. Are you assisting Inspector Derwent?"

She spun around in surprise and smiled when she saw it

was Hugo Willerby, Scotland Yard's forensic scientist, addressing her from his position on the floor beneath a large desk that dominated the room. He was a chaotic-looking young man, with red hair that stuck up at odd angles and spectacles with the thickest lenses she had ever seen.

"Hello there," she replied. "No, not exactly. My friend lives next door and she saw Mr Gaskill's body from her window and telephoned me. We thought at first he'd fallen, but now it seems clear he was killed, although Dr Stirk doesn't think it happened out in the garden."

"I agree with the doctor and if I'm not very much mistaken, he was killed while he sat here at his desk."

The young scientist clambered awkwardly out from under the desk and proudly showed Dorothy a cotton swab he was holding. There was a brownish stain in the middle of it.

"I've found this on the carpet," he explained as he removed a small glass vial from his pocket, opened it and poured the clear liquid on to the swab. "If it turns bright pink, it means it's blood."

Dorothy wrinkled her nose. "What is it? It smells dreadful."

"Hydrogen peroxide," replied Willerby just as the brown stain began to turn pink. "It's called the Kastle-Meyer test."

"Oh my goodness!" exclaimed Dorothy. "That's amazing. How clever of you."

The scientist turned as pink as the swab he was holding.

"Ah there you are, Willerby," said Inspector Derwent as he entered the room. "Have you found anything?"

"Yes, Inspector. There are bloodstains on the rug beneath his chair. Fresh, I'd say—they are still slightly damp. It looks like he was killed in here."

"Good work." He walked over to the glass-panelled door that led out to the garden. The key was still in the lock. "Have you checked the handle for fingerprints?"

"Yes," replied Willerby. "None, it's been wiped clean either by the killer or possibly the maid. The door's unlocked and I think the victim might have been dragged through and into the garden. Do you see the way the pile of the rug is lying flat?"

Both Dorothy and Inspector Derwent peered down at the two tramline marks that led to the door.

"But what about the birdseed in his hand?" asked Dorothy.

"I think that was placed there by the killer, who must have closed Gaskill's fingers together and then put in the birdseed when he was laid out in the garden," explained the inspector.

"I agree," said Willerby. "If he had truly been attacked as he was feeding the birds, he would have dropped the seed. It would be quite easy for the killer to get hold of it. It's kept in that brass urn by the door."

Dorothy looked to where he was pointing and gave a small shudder.

"How chilling! It means the killer can't have been a random burglar; it must be someone who knew his routine," she said.

"Precisely," agreed the inspector. "Also, as far as we can tell, nothing of value is missing except his watch and even though it was a gold watch, it's hardly a motive for murder. Have you found anything else, Willerby?"

"Yes. The fire must have been lit in here yesterday. I found a few remnants of paper in the grate." Willerby opened an envelope that had been lying on the desk and tipped out the contents: several scraps of charred paper.

"That looks like a wax mark," said Dorothy peering closely at the largest piece.

"I think you are right, Miss Peto," agreed Willerby. "It's rather thick paper too. I wondered if it might have been a legal document of some sort."

"Apparently, his solicitor, Mr Pearson paid him a visit yesterday."

"Strange to have a fire on such a hot day," pondered the scientist.

"Connie, the maid, said he asked her to light the fire after receiving a letter that arrived in the second post," she explained.

Inspector Derwent raised an eyebrow. "Have you already spoken to the servants, Miss Peto?" he asked. "Is that how you are aware of the solicitor's visit too?"

Dorothy shrugged her shoulders innocently. "We were just chatting. The two women were clearly upset so I made them a cup of tea."

The inspector grunted and turned back to Willerby. "Dr Stirk said he thought the victim had been struck by something with a rounded edge." He pointed to the fire irons that had heavy circular handles. "Can you test them for traces of blood?"

"Right away, Inspector," replied the scientist eagerly as he knelt down and produced another vial of hydrogen peroxide.

"Brook!" called out the inspector and one of his sergeants, a big bear of a man with a huge bushy beard, appeared in the doorway. "Bring the servants up, will you?" asked Inspector Derwent. "And be sure to do so in order of seniority—you know what they can be like. I'll talk to Duckworth first, then the cook, then the young maid."

"Yes, sir," replied the sergeant. "That should give her time to pull herself together. I only said 'good morning' and she burst into tears."

The detective disappeared and Inspector Derwent inclined his head towards Dorothy.

"Very well, Miss Peto. You can stay. Sergeants Taylor and Brook have many fine qualities but dealing with emotional maids are not amongst them."

"Thank you, Inspector," murmured Dorothy just as Duckworth entered the room.

"You wanted to see me, sir," he said.

"Yes, Mr Duckworth. Please take a seat," said the inspector.

"As you wish, sir," replied the butler. "And I should like to apologise for not being present to greet you. I had taken a moment to recover from the shock of finding Mr Gaskill."

"That's quite understandable," replied the inspector.

From her position by the desk, Dorothy watched Duckworth closely as he walked slowly and deliberately towards the armchair. He may have had the correct height and build to be a butler, but he was definitely lacking the demeanour. Nothing about him inspired confidence. His face was a little flushed and she was sure she caught the faint whiff of sherry as he passed her. Perhaps he wasn't handling the death of his master any better than his female colleagues. She took her notebook and pencil out of her pocket as the butler settled into the armchair and the inspector positioned himself in front of him.

"Can you describe the events of yesterday for us, please? Did anything out of the ordinary occur?" he asked.

The butler shook his head slowly. "No, sir. I don't believe so. It was a day like any other day. Mr Gaskill rose at half past six. He carried out his ablutions, dressed, came down to the library, went outside to feed the birds, then returned here to eat his breakfast at his desk."

Dorothy frowned as she listened. Something about the dead man's clothing was bothering her. After hearing Dr Stirk's estimated time of death, she had assumed Mr Gaskill had been disturbed in the night and come down to the library to investigate, yet he wasn't in his pyjamas.

"Mr Duckworth," she interrupted, earning herself a sharp look from the inspector, "Mr Gaskill was in his dressing gown when we found him, but I couldn't help noticing he was wearing day clothes beneath."

"That's correct, miss," replied the butler. "Mr Gaskill always wore his dressing gown over his day clothes as well as his pyjamas. He was of the opinion it protected other garments and therefore saved on laundry and general wear and tear. He always wore his slippers around the house for a similar reason. Saving on shoe leather, you understand. As I am sure you are both aware, slippers are cheaper to replace than shoes."

Dorothy nodded politely. She was beginning to think Margaret's description of Hector Gaskill not believing in extravagance was rather an understatement. It would also seem that he had been killed before retiring for the evening, so closer to ten o'clock than to four. The inspector cleared his throat.

"Mr Duckworth, I understand Mr Gaskill received a letter yesterday," he said shooting Dorothy a warning glare.

"That is correct," agreed the butler. "Various bills arrived in the first post and a letter in the second post."

"Do you know who it was from?"

The butler paused. Dorothy noticed that his eyes kept flicking to where Willerby was working in front of the fireplace.

"From the handwriting and postmark, I believed it was from Mr Paul Gaskill, Mr Gaskill's grandson, although Mr Gaskill did not say so."

"Do you know the contents of the letter?"

"Certainly not, sir," replied Duckworth sounding shocked. "I hope you aren't suggesting I read Mr Gaskill's correspondence."

"Not at all but he may have discussed it with you."

"Mr Gaskill preferred to keep both his business and personal affairs private, sir."

"I see. Was it after reading the letter that Mr Gaskill asked the maid to light the fire?"

"It was and then he asked me to send for Mr Pearson, his solicitor."

"Did you telephone him?"

"No, sir, Mr Gaskill believed the telephone was an unnecessary indulgence. I sent an errand boy with a message to Mr Pearson's office over in Holborn. Mr Pearson arrived after lunch at about three o'clock."

"And at what time did he leave?"

"A little after five o'clock. The two gentlemen remained here, in the library, the whole time."

"Do you know what they discussed?"

"I do not, sir."

"Did Mr Gaskill receive any other visitors yesterday?"

"Yes, sir. Mr Gerald arrived for supper at seven o'clock as he does every Saturday evening."

"Mr Gerald?"

"Gerald Gaskill, sir. He is the son of the master's late younger brother. They ate in the dining room then retired here to the library for their coffee and brandy."

Dorothy noticed the butler glanced over to the heavy oak sideboard where there was a silver tray holding several cut-glass decanters.

"What time did Gerald Gaskill leave?"

"At around half past ten, sir."

"And when did you last see Hector Gaskill alive?"

"At the same time. I arrived in the hall as Mr Gerald was leaving. He told me his uncle would be working on some papers for the rest of the evening and did not wish to be disturbed. I could see the master was sitting at his desk as Mr Gerald closed the library door behind him."

"So after Gerald Gaskill left, you retired for the evening?"

Duckworth shifted a little in his seat. "No, sir, I returned to my pantry. There were several matters I still needed to attend to."

"Did you hear anything unusual at all?"

"No, sir. Not a thing."

The inspector pointed to the door in the corner. "The key in the lock there, is there another one?"

"No, sir, just that one. It is always kept in the lock. The master only used that door to go into the garden and feed the birds each morning."

"What about the garden gate? That was unlocked this morning."

"It always is, sir. Mr Gaskill employed a gardener who visited once a week to mow the lawn and tend to the flower beds and such things. He didn't have a regular day; it would often depend on the weather, so the gate was left unlocked."

"Do you have a name for the gardener?"

"Yes, sir. A Mr Hurst from Fulham, but it was usually his nephew, Jack, who came here."

"I see," replied the inspector. "Mr Duckworth I appreciate it must have been a shock discovering your master's body, but have you had the opportunity to check if anything is missing? Anything of value?"

The butler shook his head. "Everything seems to be in its place, sir."

Dorothy frowned. Surely a diligent servant would want to be sure before responding so quickly, especially as theft could be a motive for their master's murder.

"And can you think of anyone who may have wished your master harm?" continued the inspector.

The butler stared at him blankly and there was just the briefest pause before he replied. "No, sir. Not a soul."

"Very well then," said the inspector. "That's all for now, Mr Duckworth. Thank you."

The butler stood up and made his way to the door, when

the inspector seemed to remember something. "One last thing, Mr Duckworth. What happened to the letter from Mr Gaskill's grandson?"

The butler turned back. "Mr Gaskill burnt it on the fire, sir."

"Was that unusual? Didn't he keep his personal correspondence?"

"He did not, sir. Mr Gaskill was not a sentimental man." And with that he left the room.

"Do you think he was telling the truth?" asked Dorothy as soon as the door clicked shut.

"About Gaskill not being sentimental? I think so, Miss Peto." He pointed to the desk and mantelpiece. "There are no family photographs anywhere to be seen, although perhaps Mr Gaskill thought they would be an unnecessary extravagance too. What about you, Willerby? I take it you haven't found anything?" he asked.

The young scientist sprang to his feet and used his handkerchief to wipe the soot and ash from his hands. "No, Inspector. No traces of blood on any of the fire irons."

"Then let us take another look at the lock. If there is truly only one key then either the door was opened by someone in the house or…"

"Someone was able to open it from the outside," Willerby interrupted eagerly, "using some sort of thin pliers perhaps. If that is the case, then the key should bear some marks or scratches."

Dorothy wandered over the sideboard while the two men were inspecting the key and began examining the decanters, carefully sniffing the contents of each one.

"Duckworth lied about one thing," she said. The two men looked around. "There's no brandy here, only whisky, sherry and port."

"Are you sure? Would you know the difference, Miss Peto?" asked the inspector.

Dorothy had to stop herself rolling her eyes. "While it is true that I'm not a hardened drinker, Inspector, my father always had a glass of brandy after dinner. I used to pour it for him. There is none here."

"And no marks on the key either," said Willerby as he carefully replaced it in the lock.

"Does that mean he must have been killed by someone who was in the house already, not an intruder?" asked Dorothy.

"It would seem so," sighed the inspector. "Let's speak to the cook. See if she can shed any light on what happened to her employer."

Chapter Three

THERE WAS A slight delay in Mrs Platt's arrival. She had been keeping herself busy providing all the policemen with tea and biscuits. When she did finally appear in the library, she arrived bearing a tray laden down with cups, saucers and scones.

"I thought you could all do with some refreshment," she said as she set the tray down on the desk. Dorothy helped her pour out the tea and Willerby immediately reached for a scone, but Inspector Derwent, who was drumming his fingers against his leg again, waved away the cup the cook offered him.

"No thank you, Mrs Platt. Would you be kind enough to take a seat."

"Oh well if you are sure, sir," she replied sitting down rather awkwardly on the sofa opposite the fireplace while the inspector began pacing up and down.

"Mrs Platt, can you tell me what Mr Gaskill ate before he died?" he began.

"Fried? Oh no, sir. Mr Gaskill never ate anything that had been fried. It didn't agree with him."

"Not fried. Died," repeated the inspector loudly. "What did he eat for supper last night?"

Dorothy raised her eyes to the ceiling. She'd warned him that the poor woman was hard of hearing.

"Last night?" Mrs Platt repeated. "Well, sir, normally Mr Gaskill liked to start with soup, but with it being so hot, I did a nice bit of salmon with a dill sauce instead. Then they had pork chops with mashed potatoes and carrots. Mr Gaskill really prefers minted new potatoes, but it isn't the time of year for them. Neither gentleman has a sweet tooth, sir, not like Mr Paul, who always enjoys my puddings, so they just finished with some cheese and biscuits. I bake my own oatmeal digestives, not those shop-bought ones some houses serve," she said proudly, then her hand suddenly flew to her mouth. "Oh my Lord! You don't think it was my cooking that did for him, do you, sir?"

"No, Mrs Platt. He died from a blow to the head."

She looked perplexed. "But he wasn't in bed, sir. He was in the garden."

Behind her, Dorothy could hear Willerby chuckling quietly.

"Oh for pity's sake," muttered the inspector.

"Don't be so impatient," chided Dorothy quietly. "She's fine as long as she can read your lips." She moved forward so she was facing the cook and knelt down next to the sofa.

"Mrs Platt, we know Mr Pearson and Mr Gaskill's nephew visited him yesterday, but did anything else out of the ordinary happen?"

The cook frowned and shook her heard.

"No, miss, not that I recall. There was a letter from Mr Paul. That made the master a bit agitated, I think."

"Agitated how?"

"It was after he received the letter that he called for Connie to light the fire and sent for his solicitor."

"I don't suppose you have any idea what was in the letter?"

"No, the master wasn't one to share personal information, which was a shame because I would have liked to have heard how Mr Paul is getting along. He's such a nice, kind, young gentleman. The house hasn't been the same since he joined up."

"You must all miss him," replied Dorothy. "But at least Mr Gaskill still had his nephew. You said he dines here regularly. Did you see him last night?"

She noticed that as she began to speak about Gerald, Mrs Platt's face hardened in the same way that Margaret's expression had changed.

"I didn't, miss. Mr Duckworth served at table and Connie cleared away."

"Then the two of you washed the dishes and went to bed."

"That's right, miss. It was about ten o'clock, our usual time."

"What about this morning? Did anything appear odd before Mr Gaskill was found?"

The cook shook her head again. "Nothing out of the ordinary. Connie was already in the kitchen when I came downstairs. It's the same every morning. We have a nice little routine. She lights the fire in the stove. Then she opens all the curtains downstairs and goes upstairs to make our beds and Mr Duckworth's while I cook breakfast. By that time, Mr Gaskill is usually downstairs. But this morning, I'd only just put the kettle on when we heard Miss Damer Dawson banging on the front door, something frightful. Mr Duckworth let her in and well you know the rest…" She trailed off.

Dorothy gave the inspector a questioning look. He had watched in silence as the two women spoke, and now he merely shook his head, so Dorothy thanked Mrs Platt for her time, helped her to her feet and handed her the much lighter tray. The cook looked delighted to see Willerby had eaten all the scones. For a skinny young man, he certainly had a good appetite.

Connie was shown in next. She had stopped crying, but her face was pale and tear-stained.

"Now, young lady, Miss Peto here tells me that Mr Gaskill asked you to light the fire after receiving a letter. Is that correct?" asked the inspector as Connie took the seat recently vacated by Mrs Platt.

"Yes, sir," she replied so quietly that Dorothy could barely hear. She had hoped the inspector would allow her to interview the maid too, but it seemed she had been relegated to merely observing and note taking again.

"It was a hot day. Did he say why he wanted a fire?"

"No, sir."

"How did he seem? Happy? Sad? Angry?"

Connie kept twisting the edge of her apron in her fingers.

"A bit upset, I'd say, sir. He had this habit of drumming his fingers on the leather top of the desk there when something was bothering him."

Dorothy smiled to herself. It sounded like Hector Gaskill

was as impatient as the inspector.

"But he didn't say anything specifically about the letter he'd received?"

"No, sir. He'd been a bit out of sorts all morning. He'd strolled to the end of the garden after feeding the birds and noticed the barges moored there. He wasn't happy. River gypsies he called them."

"I see. Now, after you'd lit the fire, did you see him burn anything on it?"

"No, sir."

"What about when Mr Pearson arrived or Mr Gerald Gaskill?"

Connie shook her head firmly. "No, sir. I didn't see neither gentlemen arrive. I was busy with my chores and then I helped Mrs Platt prepare supper for the master and Mr Gerald, but it was Mr Duckworth who served at table. I cleared at the end of the meal and saw Mr Gerald then. He told me not to worry about coming in here to draw the curtains and that he would do it, sir."

"I see. And you went to bed at the same time as Mrs Platt? About ten o'clock?"

"That's right, sir."

"You didn't hear anything in the night? Raised voices? A slamming door?"

"No nothing, sir."

"And you were the first of the servants up this morning?"

"That's not unusual, begging your pardon, sir. I'm up first every morning to light the kitchen stove and in winter, the fire in here too."

"All right. Thank you, Connie. You may go," said the inspector.

With a look of relief, the maid stood up to leave, but when she was almost at the door, she stopped and turned back. "There is one more thing, sir."

"What's that, Connie?"

"The candlesticks, sir. They're missing."

"Candlesticks?"

"Yes, sir. They are always on the windowsill behind the master's desk. Two big silver candlesticks. When it gets dark, he brings them over to the desk to read by, sir."

"Were they here yesterday?"

"Yes, sir," she replied. "I remember because I noticed the candles were getting low and I thought I would probably have to replace them today."

"Can you describe them?"

"They're about fourteen inches high with a round base and they are very heavy, sir. I could only lift one at a time."

Dorothy's ears pricked up and she quickly glanced over to Willerby who responded with an eager grin, but if the inspector shared their excitement, he wasn't showing it.

"Very well, thank you, Connie. You may go," he said with a curt nod of his head.

Connie gave Dorothy a quick smile and left the room looking only slightly less upset than when she'd arrived. Although she'd only worked for Mr Gaskill a year, Dorothy thought she seemed far more troubled by his death than the other two servants.

As soon as she'd gone, the inspector turned to Willerby who had already moved so he was now positioned between the desk and the window.

"It sounds like we may now know what the murder

weapon was. Check the sill for fingerprints," instructed the inspector.

"Certainly, Inspector, but I think the candlesticks might have been here on the desk," replied the scientist, then he suddenly bent down. "Look here on the carpet. There are tiny drops of dried wax on the rug. I didn't give them much attention before—I was focused on the bloodstain—but see how they have formed an arc." He straightened up and mimed picking up a candlestick. "Imagine someone coming behind Mr Gaskill while he was sitting at his desk, swinging the candlestick and striking him on the head. The flame would be extinguished but the wax would still be in liquid form. Dorothy knelt down to study the drops of wax close to the bloodstain.

"You're right," she agreed, then pressing her cheek against the rug she stretched her arm under the narrow gap beneath the desk drawers and felt about until her fingers closed around something smooth and cylindrical. "And here is the candle, or what's left of it. It must have rolled under here," she said as she showed them the stub of wax triumphantly.

"Oh good show, Miss Peto," exclaimed Willerby who was now using a large brush to dust powder across the windowsill.

"Brook," the inspector called out loudly and the sergeant appeared in the doorway.

"Yes, sir."

"You and Taylor start searching the house. I'm looking for a pair of large silver candlesticks. Start with the servants' bedrooms in the attic."

"Yes, sir."

"Do you think one of them killed him?" ask Dorothy. "Surely not Connie or Mrs Platt. It must be Duckworth."

The inspector simply shrugged. "We know they all had the opportunity. What we don't know is if any of them had a motive. In a murder investigation we require both."

"What about Gerald Gaskill? Are you going to speak to him?"

"No, I don't think I'll bother, Miss Peto." Then seeing her surprised face he almost smiled. "I've sent Sergeant Clark to his home address."

He began walking to the door and Dorothy felt herself flush at being teased.

"Is there anything I can do to help?" she called after him. He stopped and turned around.

"Yes, Miss Peto. You and Miss Damer Dawson can each write a statement describing what you saw this morning. As you are both members of the WPV, I'll excuse you from coming to Scotland Yard, but I should be grateful if you could let me have them as soon as possible."

"Of course, Inspector. Thank you," replied Dorothy feeling disappointed. Typing up a statement wasn't going to be half as interesting as being involved in a search or watching Willerby look for fingerprints.

Chapter Four

AFTER CALLING IN next door at number ten to tell Margaret that Inspector Derwent wanted her to make a statement, Dorothy made her way over to Little George Street, her head full of everything that had happened since that early morning phone call. However, when she arrived at the WPV offices, she was immediately distracted and delighted to find Nina sitting behind her desk.

"You're home!" she exclaimed hugging her friend. "How was the trip?"

Nina removed the ever-present cigarette from her lips and kissed Dorothy's cheek.

"Exhilarating and inspiring! It was marvellous to see so many female police volunteers throughout the country, from Newquay to Newcastle. More importantly, not merely volunteers any longer. Countless forces are recognising the contribution these women are making and are willing to pay them to support their regular constables. There have been requests to second our members as well as those who have been volunteering with the National Council of Women's patrols. Naturally, Mary wasn't happy about that. She is adamant that it should only be our members. You know how obstinate she can be."

Dorothy murmured her agreement. Their colleague had many strengths, and there was no doubting her bravery, but the word 'accommodating' was not in her vocabulary.

"I said, 'Who cares if Bristol and Bath use women from the NCW just so long as they are getting paid. That's the way we'll increase the number of women involved in policing. Not everyone can afford to work voluntarily,' but she wouldn't listen."

Dorothy glanced through into the anteroom that she and Mary used as an office.

"Where is Mary anyway?" she asked.

Nina gave her a mischievous grin. "Unfortunately, we got separated. I seem to have given her the details for the wrong train from Newcastle. There was no sign of her on my train to Grantham."

"She'll be absolutely furious," gasped Dorothy, smiling despite herself. "Where is she now?"

"Hull, I believe," replied Nina with a shrug. "I know it was naughty of me, but I simply could not endure another lecture all the way back to London. By the way, where's Margaret?"

"At home, recovering from this morning's excitement. She telephoned me in a flap to tell me she'd discovered the dead body of one of her neighbours in his garden."

"Good heavens! Was it an accident or foul play?"

"Definitely the latter. Inspector Derwent and his men are there now."

Nina gave her a knowing smile. "Are they now? Do I take it that you offered the rather striking, but oh so inscrutable inspector your assistance?"

Dorothy grinned back at her. Nina loved to tease her.

"I did as it happens. What's more, I managed to sit in while he interviewed the butler, who I think may drink, the cook, who is practically deaf, and the maid, who seemed particularly distraught."

"Excellent!"

"But then he packed me off to write up my statement," replied Dorothy with a sigh.

"Well, good for you anyway. And speaking of extraordinary occurrences, I must tell you about the most amazing person I met in Grantham. Her name is Edith Smith. She was a midwife but joined the police as a volunteer and is quite simply a force of nature. She is an outstanding personality; fearless, motherly and adaptable. Since she started working as a police volunteer, she hasn't taken a single day off and she's made such a vast difference. What's more, I think there is a chance that she could be the first woman to be attested."

Dorothy frowned and shook her head at Nina's enthusiasm, afraid that she was getting carried away as was so often the case.

"But we've looked at this before, Nina. A woman can't be given the power to arrest. The Police Acts that govern the county and borough forces only direct chief constables to swear in 'fit men' as constables. There is no references to women, fit or otherwise."

"Yes, yes, I know," replied Nina flapping her hands and sending a shower of ash from her cigarette across the desk, "but before I went away, I spent some time digging at the British Library and according to the *Special Constables Act of*

1831 full powers can be given to any fit persons, not just men. I'm about to write to Chief Inspector Casburn in Grantham and subtly inform him of my discovery." She clapped her hands together in delight, distributing yet more ash. "You know what they say, Dorothy, where there's a will, there's a way. Then I shall write to various local dignitaries: the mayor, the bishop, the local MP, his wife. I want to ensure everyone in Lincolnshire is aware of Edith and the difference she is making."

Dorothy nodded as Nina continued to excitedly explain her plans, but part of her was thinking how simply marvellous it would be if Scotland Yard decided they need to second someone from the WPV and if by some miracle they chose her. Recently, she'd been spending more and more time on administration work and less on actual policing. The number of women joining them was growing all the time and Dorothy was in charge of their enrolment and training. Even when she did go out on patrol, it was largely dealing with drunk and disorderly soldiers on leave or moving prostitutes on. The flow of refugees that had taken up so much of her time at the start of the war had now become a slow trickle. Even the Zeppelin raids that had terrified the city at the start of the summer seemed to have almost stopped.

If only she could become more involved with what she thought of as proper policing. The brief time she had spent working alongside Inspector Derwent and the other detectives had intrigued her and left her wanting to learn more from them.

She rather liked the idea of getting paid for her work too.

Fortunately, her generous father had always supported her financially, but how satisfying it would be to earn a weekly wage. To be independent and know her worth. Lucy Summerton, one of the first members of the WPV, had moved to be nearer her parents in Richmond. She had joined the NCW patrols and now earned thirty shillings a week.

"So, what do you think?" Nina interrupted her thoughts.

"Sorry?"

"I said, when I've written to Casburn and the others, shall we go to lunch at the Eustace Miles?"

"Oh, I'd love to, but I should get my statement over to Scotland Yard as soon as possible."

Nina gave her another knowing look. "And perhaps sneak a peek into the incident room and see how the investigation is coming along?"

Dorothy feigned a look of innocence. "Well, if the door happened to be open it couldn't hurt."

An hour later, Dorothy had typed up her statement. She thought she should probably wait for Margaret to arrive with hers too and so busied herself with other paperwork, occasionally glancing at the clock. It was almost four o'clock when Jean Bagster, one of the older volunteers, put her head around the door and told her that Margaret had telephoned the office to say she had come down with food poisoning after her breakfast kippers and asked if Dorothy would collect her statement tomorrow morning if she was still unwell.

Anxious not to waste any more time, Dorothy put on her hat and coat, neatly folded her statement into her pocket and hurried out the door.

When she arrived at Scotland Yard, the uniformed officer at the reception desk told her to take her statement upstairs to Sergeant Clark. She found the elderly detective in a small office, hunched over a typewriter.

She knocked softly on the open door. "Good afternoon, Sergeant. I have my statement here for you."

He looked up and groaned. "Not another one. I'm still only halfway through the butler's."

"Don't worry, Sergeant. I've already typed mine," she replied, removing the piece of paper from her pocket and carefully unfolding it.

"That's something I suppose," he grunted. "Just leave it on the pile with the others. I promised the inspector I'd have them on his desk by six."

He returned to his task, slowly typing using only one finger. It was painful to watch.

"Sergeant, why don't you let me type the statements up. It seems such a waste of your talents," she suggested gently.

The detective frowned. "I'm not sure, miss. The inspector did ask me to do it."

Dorothy glanced up at the clock. "He wouldn't need to know. I could take them up to his office along with my own when I'm done. It's already after five and I expect Mrs Clark has something delicious in the oven for your supper."

The sergeant instinctively licked his lips. "Monday night is steak and kidney pudding night. She'll not be happy if I'm late."

"Well, we can't have that, Sergeant," she replied and handed him his hat and coat with a smile.

As soon as he'd gone, Dorothy took his seat behind the

typewriter and bashed out Duckworth's statement in no time. Then she added it the neat pile with her own and carried them down the corridor to Inspector Derwent's office. His door was also open.

"Hello again, Inspector," she said brightly, placing the pile of papers on the desk. "Here are the witness statements you requested."

"Where's Clark?"

"I offered to bring you the ones he'd typed along with my own," she replied carefully. He merely grunted in reply and began flicking through the statements.

"There's no statement from Miss Damer Dawson."

"No, unfortunately she's been taken ill."

He looked up.

"Anything serious?"

"No," replied Dorothy, deciding not to elaborate, "I'll call in and collect her statement then bring it here tomorrow morning, if I may."

He nodded his acceptance and turned his attention back to the statements. "In your statement, you say that Duckworth went for 'a breath of air' before we arrived, while you were in the kitchen with the maid and the cook."

"That's correct. You'll recall he apologised for not being there to greet you."

"Did he say where he was going?"

"No, I assumed he was upset, but being male and the senior member of the household, didn't want to let it show in front of myself or Connie and Mrs Platt. I thought it odd he left when he knew you were on your way, but as he implied, he may have needed a moment to compose himself."

He raised an eyebrow but said nothing.

"Did you manage to find the silver candlesticks when you searched the house?" she asked quickly before he could dismiss her.

"No, we did not."

"Perhaps the killer took them with him."

"If they are indeed missing."

"Why do you say that? Connie seemed very sure."

"Unfortunately, Connie—along with the other two servants—aren't what I would describe as the most credible of witnesses."

"What do you mean?"

He looked up from reading her statement.

"As we've already established Mrs Platt is practically deaf. A whole battalion could have marched through the house the night her employer was killed, and I doubt she would have heard it. And although we did not find the missing candlesticks, we did discover plenty of other things when we searched the servants' rooms in the attic. Judging by the number of empty bottles and torn-up betting slips we found under Duckworth's bed, I'd say he is both a gambler and a drinker. We discovered the missing brandy decanter in his pantry. It was also empty. I'd be surprised if he was conscious let alone sober when Hector Gaskill was killed."

Dorothy nodded. She'd been right when she'd thought she'd smelt alcohol on his breath.

"And Connie Beal?"

"Miss Beal is a liar."

"No!" exclaimed Dorothy in surprise. "What on earth makes you think that?"

"When we went into her bedroom it was obvious that she hadn't slept in her bed. I'm sure you remember, Mrs Platt had already told us the servants' daily routines. Connie makes all the beds after the breakfast things have been cleared away. As soon as I asked her about this, she burst into tears again. Eventually, she admitted that she hadn't spent the night at the house, but I couldn't get any more sense out of her."

Dorothy pursed her lips. She had to stop herself saying that if he'd allowed her to stay, she might have been able to find out why the young maid had lied.

"There could be a perfectly innocent explanation."

"I agree, but the point is, when questioned by a senior police officer, she lied. And there's more. You'll recall one of my men found something just before you and Miss Damer Dawson rounded up her chaotic canines."

"Yes, by the birdbath."

"The birdbath stands in a patch of soil and in that soil we discovered two footprints. Apparently, Mr Gaskill insisted the birdbath was filled every day, and sometimes the water overflowed. It created the only damp patch of earth in the whole garden. The first footprint was clearly a man's, but the other was smaller and an exact match for Connie's shoes."

Dorothy began to shake her head. She could hardly believe what he was saying. The young woman had seemed genuinely distraught. If it was an act, then she deserved to be on the stage.

"Surely you don't think that means she could be involved in Mr Gaskill's death somehow? That doesn't make any sense. If she was, why would she draw our attention to the missing candlestick?"

The inspector gave a heavy sigh.

"Miss Peto, I gave up trying to understand the criminal mind long ago. As I explained in the library, whenever I begin investigating a murder, I look for two things: opportunity and motive. Currently, I have plenty of one and none of the other. However, I'm expecting a visit from Mr Pearson, Mr Gaskill's solicitor. Hopefully, he may be able to furnish us with the information we require."

At that moment, there was a knock on the door.

"Come in," called out the inspector.

Sergeant Brook put his head around the door. "Mr Pearson is here to see you, sir."

"Thank you, Brook. Show him in."

The inspector rose to his feet and Dorothy did the same, assuming she would be asked to leave while the inspector spoke with the solicitor. Arnold Pearson stepped awkwardly around the bulk of Sergeant Brook. He was a short, bespectacled man, as wide as he was tall with an open, cheerful, ruddy face and greying curly hair.

"Good afternoon, Inspector Derwent," he began sounding a little breathless as he plonked his bulging bag down on the desk. "Forgive me for the delay. I only received your message a little while ago. I was in church this morning, then I returned to my office to collect some papers I intended to read this evening."

The inspector reached out and shook his hand. "Not at all, Mr Pearson. Thank you for coming." Then seeing the solicitor give Dorothy a smile: "This is Miss Peto, a member of the Women Police Volunteers. She and Miss Damer Dawson, Mr Gaskill's neighbour, discovered the deceased."

"Good heavens. That must have been terribly upsetting for you. Do please take a seat, young lady."

Dorothy murmured her thanks and threw Inspector Derwent a questioning look. In return he gave a nod of resignation and they all sat down.

"Please accept my condolences on the death of your client," he began.

The solicitor removed his glasses and began polishing them with his large spotty handkerchief. "Thank you, Inspector. I must say it was quite a shock. I truly thought Hector would outlive us all. He seemed to have the constitution of an ox!"

"I'm afraid he did not die of natural causes. We believe Mr Gaskill was murdered."

The solicitor replaced his glasses and stared at the inspector, seemingly dumbfounded. Dorothy noticed his fingers were stained with ink and one of his jacket buttons was hanging loose on just a few threads. She would be very surprised if Mr Pearson wasn't a bachelor.

"Who on earth would want to do such a thing, Inspector?" he finally stammered.

"We were hoping you might be able to tell us, Mr Pearson. Had you known Mr Gaskill long?"

"Oh yes indeed, Inspector. He'd been my client for over twenty years and my father's client before me."

"How would you describe him?"

The solicitor paused, giving the question serious consideration. "A shrewd, intelligent businessman, who didn't suffer fools gladly." Then he exhaled and shook his head. "However, if I had to use one word, Inspector. It would be cantankerous. I know it is wrong of me to speak ill of the dead, but Hector Gaskill was not an easy client. God rest his soul."

"Such a man may acquire enemies. Can you think of anyone who would wish him harm?"

"No, no. Absolutely not."

"I understand he sent for you yesterday afternoon."

"That is correct. He wanted to update his will."

"Did he often amend his will?" asked Dorothy, thinking of one of her maiden aunts who was known to constantly tinker with hers depending on which friend or relation was in or out of favour.

"Not at all, Miss Peto. The last time was nine years ago, when he lost his son and daughter-in-law. They died out in India, you know. Terribly sad."

"What were the contents of this new will?" asked the inspector.

The solicitor looked uncomfortable. "I hope you don't mind, Inspector, while it is true that I am the executor of Mr Gaskill's estate, I would prefer to wait until the formal reading of the will. In order to do that, I shall of course need to retrieve the will from Mr Gaskill's library."

"We found no will in the library or anywhere else in twelve Cheyne Row," replied the inspector.

The solicitor turned quite pale. "Oh good Lord, Inspector, are you sure?"

"Quite sure, sir."

"Well, well, we must find it," stammered the solicitor. "A

man like Hector Gaskill can't die intestate. I'll be a laughingstock around the inns of court."

"Intestate?" queried Dorothy. She'd never heard the term before.

"It means to die without a will," explained the inspector as Mr Pearson became more and more agitated.

"What about the old will, Mr Pearson? Couldn't you revert to that?" asked Dorothy.

The solicitor shook his head. "Null and void, Miss Peto, null and void. You see Mr Gaskill refused to pay for a completely new will to be drawn up and insisted on retaining the first few pages of the old will. However, he removed the page containing the now obsolete bequests and the final page of signatures and threw them on to the fire. Then he asked me to add the new instructions and a new last page for the new date, signature and witnesses."

"And what were these new instructions, Mr Pearson?" asked the inspector. Dorothy could hear the edge of impatience creeping into his voice.

"That his entire estate should go to Paul Gaskill, his grandson."

"And why was that different from his first will?"

"In that will, the bulk of his fortune still went to Paul, but there was also generous provision for Gerald, his nephew, and Emily, his ward. In addition, his servants also received bequests for their loyal service. Not huge amounts, but enough for the older two to retire and live modestly."

"May I ask the value of Mr Gaskill's estate?"

Mr Pearson puffed out his cheeks and waggled his head from side to side. "I can't give you an exact figure, you understand, Inspector, but taking into consideration, the house in Cheyne Row, his investments, the stocks and shares in his portfolio, and his other business interests, I would say in the area of one hundred thousand pounds."

"Gosh," murmured Dorothy. Such a vast sum of money could certainly be the motive the inspector was looking for. However, as usual, he hadn't shown any visible reaction to what the solicitor had said; instead he continued to pursue his line of questioning.

"Did Mr Gaskill say what had prompted him to make this change to his will? We understand he received a letter before he sent for you. Did he mention that at all?"

"No he didn't, Inspector. He wasn't one for explaining his actions. There were a few comments about ensuring his bloodline continued to prosper and that everything he'd worked for was not to be frittered away on wastrels. That sort of thing, but nothing specific. Oh dear, I do hope you can find the will, Inspector."

He began mopping his brow with his spotty handkerchief.

Dorothy felt a pang of sympathy. "Isn't there a copy anywhere?" she asked.

He turned to her look at her and shook his head. "Copies cost money, Miss Peto. Mr Gaskill saw it as unnecessary extravagance. 'Why do I need a copy, Pearson?' he'd say. 'Is your firm in the habit of losing important legal documents? If that is the case, perhaps I should take my business elsewhere'."

"May I ask why didn't you take the new will back to your office with you?" enquired the inspector.

"A will requires two witnesses, Inspector. I was the first witness and I believe he was going to ask his nephew, Gerald Gaskill, to be the second witness, then send Duckworth around with it in the morning. Don't either of those gentlemen know where the will is?"

"Mr Duckworth does not recall seeing the document at all. And, as yet, we haven't been able to ascertain the whereabouts of Mr Gerald Gaskill. One of my men paid a visit to his home address but he wasn't there. His wife said she hadn't seen him for some time."

"Oh dear, that must have been very upsetting for poor Emily." Mr Pearson quickly got to his feet. "I should go and offer her my condolences." He started heading towards the door, but the inspector stopped him.

"Hold on a moment please, Mr Pearson. Surely both yourself and Gerald Gaskill would have needed to be present at the same time if you were to witness Hector Gaskill signing the will."

The solicitor's face turned bright red. "Yes Inspector, that is the normal convention. However, as I explained, Hector could be extremely difficult. He saw no need to have two signatories, but I absolutely insisted. 'Very well, Pearson,' he said, 'I'll get Gerald to witness it, but I won't pay for you to loiter here any longer. My nephew knows my signature well enough without needing to watch me scribbling like a child'," the solicitor was almost stammering. "Inspector, you must understand, Hector could be rather cruel. I can quite imagine he would enjoy asking his nephew to sign a document that would make him much poorer. No doubt, he thought it would teach him a lesson." He pushed the door open, then glanced over his shoulder. "If I were you, Inspector, I'd try to locate Gerald by searching the city's least reputable drinking establishments. Good day and do please let me know if you find the will."

Then with a polite nod of the head to them both, he hurried out the door, repeating, "Dear me, dear me," under his breath.

"The poor man," said Dorothy, but the inspector merely tutted and shook his head. "You don't think Mr Pearson deserves my sympathy?" she asked.

"I don't think Mr Pearson acted in the best interest of his client and that's being charitable."

"You can't blame him. Hector Gaskill sounds rather a bully."

"Perhaps, Miss Peto, but if Mr Pearson had been a stronger man and insisted on a second copy or keeping the will in his possession, Mr Gaskill may still be alive."

"You think you have your motive?"

"I do."

The inspector turned his attention back to the statements on his desk and Dorothy shook her head sadly. "And all because he didn't want to pay for a second copy of his last will and testament."

"I believe it's what is known as a false economy. Would you be so kind as to close the door on your way out, Miss Peto?"

Chapter Five

DOROTHY RELUCTANTLY LEFT Scotland Yard and made her way home to Bloomsbury. It was still oppressively hot, but the sky was leaden and in the distance, there was a rumble of thunder. It was almost seven o'clock when she arrived at the door to her flat, over twelve hours since she'd received Margaret's telephone call, but it felt an awful lot longer.

She put her hand on the handle, then paused. Inside she could hear music playing. Carefully, she twisted the handle. It was unlocked. She pushed it open and cautiously stepped inside and tiptoed down the hallway to the sitting room. Now she recognised the tune. It was 'They Didn't Believe Me' playing on the gramophone. As she stepped into the sitting room, she found her brother was slumped at the table, a bottle of whisky half empty in front of him.

"Raymond!" she exclaimed hurrying towards him. "What are you doing here?"

"My commanding officer has given me seventy-two hours' leave."

"Why? Has something happened?"

"George is dead."

Dorothy stared at him in stunned silence for a second.

"George? George Sledmere? No. He can't be," she stammered.

"A new offensive began yesterday morning, near a place called Loos. We managed to break through the enemy lines but there were supply and communication problems. The infantry suffered heavy losses. I was one of the first to see the casualty list. George's name was on it." Dorothy watched in horror as her brother's face crumpled. "How can he be dead? He was my best friend, Dorothy."

She flung her arms around him and held him as he sobbed into her shoulder. She'd known George for years. He and Raymond had met when they were thirteen, on their first day at school, and had been practically inseparable. She'd lost count of the number of holidays he'd spent with their family in Hampshire. How could he be gone?

When his sobs finally subsided, Raymond pulled away, ran his hand across his face and threw back another slug of whisky.

"Would you like me to make you a cup of tea instead?" she offered, but he shook his head and got unsteadily to his feet.

"No thanks, old girl. I'm going to my room. I need to leave for Yorkshire in the morning, get there before the telegram. I should be the one to tell his mother and help sort out his affairs. It's what he would have wanted. Goodnight."

With that he picked up the glass and bottle and staggered out of the room. Dorothy stared after him, as her own tears steadily rolled down her face. Raymond had worked for the Foreign Office, but when war broke out, he'd begun working for Sir Vernon Kell in his newly formed military intelligence section. His work was highly secretive. She barely heard from him and had been longing to see him, but not like this, so shocked and saddened.

As for poor George, she'd seen him a couple of months ago. The last time she'd seen him, he'd presented her with a huge bouquet of roses. He'd been a suspect in the case of the two actresses who had died in suspicious circumstances and had wanted to thank her for helping convince Inspector Derwent, he'd got the wrong man. She'd been in such a rush that day, she'd barely thanked him or said goodbye. Now she'd never see him again. If only she could go back to that moment and hug him and tell him how much he meant to her and her family. Lovely, kind, easy-going George had actually said he was looking forward to getting back to the front. Dorothy wiped away her tears.

She stood up and switched off the gramophone. George had loved music. He was always singing the latest tunes, completely off-key of course. Taking a deep breath, she switched off the lights, picked up the oil lamp from the table and followed Raymond down the corridor to her own room.

WHEN SHE WOKE the next morning, she found a note from her brother, telling her that he had already left for Yorkshire. Leaning against the kitchen dresser, sipping her cup of tea, she wondered how Raymond would possibly find the words to tell the recently widowed Lady Sledmere that she had now lost her only son and heir too. She cleared away Raymond's whisky glass and the remnants of his hasty breakfast. Normally she couldn't wait to go to work, but this morning she was in no rush.

When she finally left the flat, she headed to Chelsea as she had done the previous morning, although this time she walked the whole way there. She couldn't shake the heavy cloak of sadness that had settled on her shoulders. George wasn't the only young man to have lost his life. She'd heard stories of schools holding special morning assemblies to read out the names of old boys who only months ago had been sitting for exams or playing cricket but were now dead. At town halls, the names of the fallen were read out during council meetings and each London borough was displaying rolls of honour to commemorate the young men they had lost. It felt like death was everywhere and now she had to collect Margaret's statement regarding Hector Gaskill.

However, when she arrived at ten Cheyne Row, it wasn't Margaret waiting for her in the drawing room but Mary.

"Oh hello, you're back," she said as Mary, dressed, even though she wasn't on duty, in the uniform of the WPV, unfolded her tall, angular frame from the sofa and strode over to shake Dorothy's hand.

"I am, no thanks to Nina! I should have been home yesterday; instead I found myself on a train to Hull of all places. I had to travel all through the night to get home. What was she thinking?"

"Oh you know how disorganised she can be when it comes to travel arrangements," replied Dorothy quickly, keen not to get drawn into what was bound to be another disagreement between Mary and Nina. "How is Margaret?"

"Still in bed suffering, the dear old girl." Mary placed her hands firmly on her hips. "And that's another thing. If I'd been here, I could have warned her about the kippers. They are such a favourite of hers, she always overindulges."

Dorothy nodded sympathetically. "Has she felt strong enough to write her statement regarding poor Mr Gaskill?"

"She has. She dictated as I typed." Mary handed over an envelope with Inspector Derwent's name printed neatly on the front. "And no more of this poor Mr Gaskill nonsense, Dorothy. He was a ghastly man," she declared decisively. "A terrible penny-pincher. It was like living next door to Ebenezer Scrooge. Margaret had a soft spot for him because he always fed the birds and made a fuss of the dogs when he saw them. All I can say is, it's a pity he didn't treat his servants so well. Dismissing that poor young maid rather than track down the scoundrel who got her into trouble. And she wasn't the first. Then marrying innocent little Emily to that bounder nephew of his. No, I'm sorry, Dorothy, but I shan't shed a tear for him."

Dorothy nodded again. She was used to Mary not mincing her words.

"I should probably be going now. I promised Inspector Derwent that I would hand over Margaret's statement this morning."

"Then I'll have Annie get Tippitt to drive you there. You had better take this too." Mary handed over a telegram addressed to Hector Gaskill. "He's dead, I'm afraid. Poor young chap. Killed in action."

Dorothy stared at her. Was she talking about: Hector or George?

"Who? Why do you have a telegram for?" she asked in

confusion.

Mary's hands returned to her hips as she tutted irritably. "Paul Gaskill. Hector's grandson. There was another battle. The papers are calling it the Battle of Loos. The telegram arrived this morning. Duckworth didn't know what to do, so he came over to ask Margaret's advice. As she is incapacitated, I deputised for her in her role as commandant of the Women Police Volunteers and opened it myself. Inspector Derwent is probably the chap to hand it to now. He can decide if it is relevant to the case."

"Thank you," replied Dorothy thinking that Paul may well have died alongside George, then immediately wondering if there could possibly be a connection between the death of grandfather and grandson. She slipped the telegram and envelope into her pocket as Annie appeared in the doorway.

"Ah, Annie, there you are. Tell Tippitt to drive Miss Peto to Scotland Yard, would you?"

"Yes, sir," replied the maid, bobbing a curtsey.

Dorothy followed the maid downstairs and wondered if she would ever get used to Mary being addressed as 'sir' by Margaret's servants.

Thanks to Margaret's excellent driver, Dorothy reached Scotland Yard in no time. As she made her way to the inspector's office, Hugh Willerby and Sergeant Clark were heading down the corridor towards her.

"Hello there, Miss Peto. What brings you to Scotland Yard?" asked Willerby greeting her with a huge smile.

"I'm delivering Miss Damer Dawson's statement regarding Mr Gaskill to the inspector. She's been indisposed."

"Oh I am sorry. Nothing serious I hope."

"Some kippers she had for breakfast yesterday. They disagreed with her," she explained.

The scientist nodded thoughtfully. "Ah yes. Scombroid fish poisoning occurs when there are high levels of histamine present. It can cause quite nasty symptoms like nausea, skin rashes…"

"Come now! I don't think this charming young lady wants to hear all the gory details, old chap," interrupted the man lounging across two of the wooden chairs in the corridor. Dorothy had been so deep in thought, she hadn't noticed him until now. He was wearing evening dress with his tie undone and his top hat and cane resting on a third chair. His blond hair flopped into his blue eyes and he had high cheekbones that Dorothy imagined many women would find attractive, but she thought his mouth looked thin and cruel. However, this didn't stop him giving her a lecherous smile.

"Allow me to introduce myself, my dear. I'm Gerald Gaskill." When she ignored his outstretched hand, he patted the seat next to him. "Now why don't you take a seat here and tell me what a pretty girl like you is doing in that awfully dowdy uniform?"

"I'd keep walking if I were you, miss," murmured Sergeant Clark, giving her a meaningful look.

Dorothy was about to do just that, when the office door opened and out stepped Inspector Derwent. He raised an eyebrow. "I wasn't aware that we had begun holding meetings in corridors now."

"Sorry, sir," muttered Clark.

"Just on my way now, Inspector," agreed Willerby and

both men scurried away.

Gerald Gaskill was on his feet too now. "About time, Inspector. I've been waiting here for over ten minutes," he drawled.

The inspector ignored him. "Miss Peto, how may I help you?" he asked instead.

"I have Miss Damer Dawson's statement for you," she replied handing the envelope to the inspector.

"Damer Dawson. I know that name. Isn't she Uncle Hector's neighbour? Lives with that terrible Allen woman. I'd rather like to hear what the old trout has to say too," said the man, who Dorothy now knew was Hector Gaskill's nephew.

Inspector Derwent looked him up and down, his expression even grimmer than usual. "Would the two of you be kind enough to step into my office, please?"

Dorothy did as he asked and sat down on the chair he silently offered her. Gerald strolled in after her. He sat down and lit a cigarette without asking permission to do either.

The inspector took his seat behind the desk. "Mr Gaskill, it has taken my men over twenty-four hours to locate you. Now you are here, may I offer my condolences on the death of your uncle."

Gerald gave a casual shrug. "An elderly wealthy man was bound to be a target for the criminals that roam our city, especially one who was careless about locking doors and gates. I told him a hundred times he should be more cautious, especially now you police are so understaffed. Law-abiding taxpayers can't rely on you for protection. Can't say I'm going to hold my breath waiting for you and your bunch of plods to catch his killer."

The inspector ignored the jibe. "I understand you dined with your uncle on Saturday evening."

"I did."

"And while you were there you witnessed his will."

Gerald blew a long plume of smoke across the room. "Is that what it was? I signed something, but I assumed it was for some business document. A share certificate or stock transfer."

"No, sir, it was for the new will that his solicitor had drawn up that afternoon. We would very much like to locate this will. Do you happen to know where your uncle put it?"

"In his desk in the library, I expect. I really wasn't paying much attention."

"It isn't there. My officers searched the house thoroughly."

Gerald seemed to find this amusing. "Get a copy from Pearson then."

"Mr Gaskill insisted only one will was drawn up. Mr Pearson does not have a copy."

"That doesn't surprise me. The man is a complete imbecile. He was always letting Uncle Hector push him around, never standing up to him. I suppose he'll just have to revert to the previous will. I can't imagine the two documents were very different."

"Mr Pearson tells me the previous will was destroyed."

Gerald sat bolt upright so quickly, he made Dorothy jump. "What?" he snapped, his eyes flashing with anger.

"There is no valid last will and testament for Hector Gaskill," the inspector explained calmly.

"If he died without a will, then the next of kin automatically gets everything. The boy soldier gets the lot." He was almost spitting out the words. "All because of Pearson. The incompetent bloody idiot!"

Inspector Derwent glared at him. "I would ask you to check your language in front of a lady, please, sir. When we couldn't find you, we thought you may have returned to your regiment or been sent abroad even. However, I take it by your current attire, you have not enlisted, sir?"

Gerald's lips twisted into a sneer as he stubbed out his cigarette. "Volunteer to be cannon fodder? No fear! I'll leave that to fools like Paul. He can play at being a hero if he wants, but I plan to stay on this side of the Channel for as long as possible."

Despite herself, Dorothy could feel tears welling up in her eyes. Only last night, she found herself wishing that George and Raymond had stayed out of the war, not put themselves in danger. She'd been thinking what this horrid man was saying.

"Is everything all right, Miss Peto?" enquired the inspector, who was watching her intently.

She rapidly blinked away the tears. "Actually, I have some news regarding Mr Paul Gaskill too, Inspector." She fished the telegram out of her pocket and handed it over. "It arrived this morning. Duckworth didn't know what to do, so he took it to Margaret and Mary."

"What does it say? Is he injured?" asked Gerald, leaning forward to try to get a look at the telegram.

"He's dead," replied the inspector.

"Hector and Paul both dead!" exclaimed Gerald. His expression had completely changed from fury to joy, and he could barely keep the glee out of his voice. "That is a turn-up for the books. It looks like this is my lucky day after all, Inspector. You are looking at the only Gaskill male still standing. The sole heir to the old man's fortune," he crowed. He was making Dorothy feel quite queasy and Inspector Derwent looked disgusted.

"You will have to take that up with Mr Pearson," he replied, "but I think you'll find it extremely difficult to inherit with your head in the hangman's noose, sir."

Gerald's smile vanished again. "What the devil do you mean, Derwent?"

"Your uncle was found murdered yesterday morning after altering his will. A will that he asked you to witness."

"Hold on, hold on. He was alive when I left him. You ask Duckworth. And I told you, he didn't tell me what he was signing. He was a bloody secretive old sod."

The inspector turned to Dorothy. "Miss Peto, perhaps you would be kind enough to take this telegram to Mr Pearson. I'm sure he will find it of interest."

"Of course, Inspector," she replied, more than happy to have an excuse to leave.

"No need to hurry off on my account," she heard Gerald call after her.

She gave a shudder as she walked away. What an utterly despicable man!

Chapter Six

M R PEARSON'S OFFICES were as small, messy and welcoming as the man himself. Potted plants interspaced the heavy legal tomes on the bookshelves and there were two canaries tweeting in a large cage in once corner. A heavy oak desk was almost totally covered in piles of legal documents and on the windowsill behind this desk was a collection of silver-framed photographs.

"Are those your children, Mr Pearson?" she enquired taking a seat in one of the large comfortable leather armchairs while the solicitor fussed around trying to tidy and asking Dennis, his elderly clerk, to see they were not interrupted.

"Dear me, no, Miss Peto," he replied with a chuckle. "I'm afraid I have never been fortunate enough to marry; however, I am honoured to be godfather to these lovely young people. Six in total. Three boys and three girls."

Dorothy smiled as he squeezed into his own seat, and she wondered who the young woman in the seventh photo was. She looked to be in her early twenties. She had a pretty face, but it was half covered by a port wine birthmark.

"Now how may I help you, Miss Peto?" he enquired.

"I'm afraid I have more bad news, Mr Pearson," she replied handing the telegram over. "This arrived at twelve

Cheyne Row today. Mr Duckworth didn't know what to do with it, so I took it to Inspector Derwent and he suggested I bring it here."

The solicitor nodded as his eyes scanned the brief message and the cheery smile faded and his shoulders drooped.

"Oh dear, oh dear," he murmured sadly. "Poor, poor Paul. Such a lovely young man with his whole life ahead of him. To think the last time I saw him, we were toasting his good health on his twenty-first birthday."

Dorothy remembered something Margaret had said to her. "Was that about the same time as the wedding of Mr Gaskill's ward to Gerald Gaskill?"

The solicitor's face clouded as he reached behind him for the photograph of the young woman with the birthmark that Dorothy had been wondering about. He placed the photograph carefully on the desk.

"Yes, this is his ward, Emily Judd. Emily is a lovely young woman, very well read and a gifted pianist. She does a great deal of good work with the Women's Institute and for her church. Her mother died when she was only a baby and her father…" he paused "…I'm sorry to say he took his own life when Emily was thirteen."

"How dreadful," gasped Dorothy. "What on earth made him do such a thing?"

"He lost a great deal of money. I don't know all the details, I'm afraid. He had been in partnership with Hector. When he died, Hector took Emily in."

He carefully replaced Emily's photograph on the windowsill.

"It was Hector's idea that she should marry Gerald. He

thought marriage might calm Gerald down and, as Hector rather cruelly put it, Emily didn't exactly have suitors queuing up."

Dorothy frowned. She couldn't imagine a man as selfish and shallow as Gerald marrying someone with what she was sure he would consider a disfigurement. Why would he have agreed to it?

"Did Miss Judd have a dowry?" she enquired.

"No, all her family's money was gone, but I believe Hector gave her a very generous wedding gift of fifty guineas. Although he did rather spoil it by saying it was cheaper than feeding and clothing her for the rest of her life."

"Is Gerald Gaskill a wealthy man?"

"His father left him an annuity, which if he budgeted carefully would give him a comfortable life, but 'budget' and 'careful' are not words in Gerald's vocabulary. I'm afraid he lives beyond his means."

Dorothy could well believe it.

"I met him this morning at Scotland Yard," she said.

The solicitor looked surprised. "So the police have finally tracked him down, have they? It seems they had more success than Emily. She's been trying to find him since she heard about Hector."

He stood up and began pacing the floor in front of the birdcage.

"Gerald said Hector didn't tell him what he was signing. Do you think that's true?" she asked.

"Oh quite possibly. Hector was extremely secretive," he replied pausing in front of the cage as the two canaries tweeted at him.

"What happens to Mr Gaskill's estate now?" asked Dorothy.

He sighed deeply and turned towards her. "Well now, Miss Peto, that rather depends on exactly when Paul died. The telegram doesn't tell us that. If he died before his grandfather, then Gerald—as the closest living relative—inherits everything. However, if it can be proved that Paul died after his grandfather, then even under the rules of intestate, Paul would have inherited, albeit briefly, and everything would go to the beneficiaries of his will, assuming he made one."

"But you don't know if he did? He didn't ask you to draw up a will when he came of age or enlisted?"

The solicitor shook his head. "No, he did not. I have to say, the whole business is extremely troubling. Now if you will excuse me, Miss Peto, I must go to Emily and break yet more bad news. She'll be devastated. She was very fond of Paul."

Dorothy rose to her feet. "Of course, Mr Pearson. Thank you for your time."

"Not at all, Miss Peto. Thank you."

Rather than going home or back to the WPV offices, Dorothy found herself wandering towards Trafalgar Square and before she knew it, she was standing on the steps of the National Gallery. She had often visited the place as a child with her father, who was an artist himself. It was somewhere that always filled her with a sense of calm and after all the upset of the last twenty-four hours, that was exactly what she needed.

She strolled through the vast hallways, enjoying the peace

and quiet. Her father, who was a landscape artist, used to bring her here to show her his favourite paintings. He was a huge admirer of Turner and Constable. Dorothy preferred the French impressionists. She stopped in their room, found an empty bench and spent an hour gazing at the Manets and Renoirs in silence. She found herself thinking about George and the death of the two Gaskills.

Her mind began sifting through everything she'd been told. What Mary had said about Emily's marriage seemed to match with what Mr Pearson had told her. And she'd said something about a maid being dismissed. Dorothy had been so lost in her own grief for George, that she hadn't given what Mary was saying her full attention. Now she wished she had pressed her further. It was unlike Mary to gossip, so there must be some truth in what she had said. Could what had happened to previous maids, be the reason why Connie had lied? It bothered her to think she'd misjudged the maid. She had believed she was full of grief for her master, when really she was worried about her own situation.

Feeling cross with herself, Dorothy stood up and made her way back through the hallways and corridors. The doorman tipped his cap to her as she left. Dorothy smiled in return but couldn't help thinking that only a year ago he might not have been so polite. The gallery had been closed to the public following a protest by one of her fellow suffragettes, although Dorothy herself had been appalled at the idea of slashing paintings. As she made her way back down the steps, she stopped in her tracks. There was Inspector Derwent striding across Trafalgar Square.

"Hello there!" she called out. He stopped and turned to

look at her in surprise.

"Hello again, Miss Peto," he replied, raising his hat.

"Are you an art lover too?" she asked.

"What?" he asked. Then as if noticing the gallery for the first time, shook his head. "No. Or rather I am but that isn't the reason I'm here. I'm on my way to check if Gerald Gaskill's alibi holds water. He told me after he left his uncle, he spent the rest of the night at Ciro's club."

"The whole night?"

"Until about half past two or three o'clock."

"Then did he go home?"

"Apparently not."

"Gosh, I wonder what his wife had to say about that," she said falling into step with the inspector who had begun walking again. "I saw a photograph of her at Mr Pearson's office earlier. I certainly wouldn't have put the two of them together."

Inspector Derwent didn't respond to this piece of information so Dorothy pressed on.

"Mr Pearson also told me that Gerald would indeed inherit everything, if it turns out Paul died before his grandfather. I can't say I like that idea one bit, but if Paul did die after his grandfather, there's nothing to say he made a will, so Gerald will probably inherit either way."

"I'd be extremely surprised if Paul hadn't made a will. Soldiers are usually told to make sure their affairs are in order before they go into battle. I know I was," the inspector replied. Dorothy glanced up at him. He rarely referred to his part in the Boer War. The injuries he received there had left him with the scar on his face and the need to walk with a stick, but his face was now as impassive as ever. She waited to see if he would elaborate further. He did not.

"If that's the case, who do you think he would have left all his worldly goods to? Oh, I do hope it isn't Gerald. What do you think, Inspector?"

"I don't know, Miss Peto; perhaps we could address that question after we discover who killed Hector Gaskill."

Dorothy noted the hint of sarcasm but pressed on regardless. "Has Dr Stirk been able to give a more accurate time of death?"

"No. He's still saying between ten o'clock and four the next morning."

"That's not terribly helpful. We know Gerald didn't leave until half past ten."

"Quite."

They turned on to Orange Street and stopped in front of a door with a black awning bearing the name *Ciro's* in gold letters. The inspector was about to raise his hat and say 'goodbye' so Dorothy quickly pre-empted him.

"May I join you?" she asked eagerly.

He studied her for a moment. "I'm not sure, Miss Peto. From what I've heard, Ciro's really doesn't sound like the sort of place that would be suitable for a young lady such as yourself to visit."

Dorothy put her hands on her hips. "Come now, Inspector. I've been patrolling the streets of London almost every evening for the best part of a year; I doubt there is much that could shock me and, who knows, I might be of some use. Two pairs of eyes and ears are better than one."

"Very well, but don't say I didn't warn you," he replied

with a shrug as he pushed open the door and set off again at his usual brisk pace, his stick taping rhythmically on the steps that led down into the nightclub. Dorothy hurried after him, wondering what Ciro's and its clientele would be like. Many of the city's clubs had been forced to close as so many men had heeded Kitchener's call to join up.

However, as soon as her eyes adjusted to the dimly lit, cigarette-smoke-filled interior, Dorothy got the distinct impression that Ciro's clientele wouldn't concern themselves with fulfilling their patriotic duty. A polished chrome bar took up the whole of one wall while red velvet banquettes lined the other walls. There was a large dance floor with a raised platform where a band were playing, even at this hour of the day. Dorothy recognised the tune. It was 'The Memphis Blues'. Raymond had brought the gramophone recording back with him after a trip to New York the year before. He and George thought it was marvellous, but Dorothy wasn't at all sure about this strange modern style of music that didn't seem to have any structure. The first time she'd heard it, Raymond and George had been joking around in the flat and they had attempted to teach her the new way of dancing they'd witnessed in America.

She watched now as several scantily clad young women gyrated wildly around a couple of older men in evening dress. They looked as dishevelled as Gerald. No wonder he had spent the night here. He would fit in perfectly.

The inspector stood on the edge of the dance floor. His eyes were scanning the room.

"Are you looking for someone in particular?" asked Dorothy.

"The proprietor," he replied, "Mr Eric Curtis. Previously Mr Eric Curtis, King's Counsel, before he was disbarred."

"A barrister owns this place?" she asked incredulously.

"One who used to represent most of the city's criminal fraternity. It seems he preferred their interpretation of the law rather than the judiciary's. According to Gerald Gaskill, he and Curtis are old friends. They met when they were both studying law."

"Don't tell me Gerald is a lawyer too? I don't believe it."

"No. It seems halfway through the course, he decided a career in law wasn't for him. He felt the same way about stockbroking and banking apparently, but remained friends with Curtis throughout."

"Do you know Curtis?"

"Our paths crossed several times during his previous career. Now occasionally we find he can be useful to us."

Dorothy's ears pricked up. She'd heard the inspector and his men discuss various informants they used, but she'd never met any of them. It sounded like Eric Curtis might be one.

"Ah, there he is."

Dorothy followed the inspector across the dance floor to the other side of the room, where a man was lounging on one of the velvet banquettes. Like Gerald, he was wearing evening dress, although he looked decidedly smarter than his friend. His dark hair was slicked back, and his hooded eyes were studying the newspaper on the table in front of him. As they got closer Dorothy could see it was the racing page of *The Sportsman.* He looked up when he heard the inspector's footsteps and the tapping of his cane.

"Derwent! To what do I owe the pleasure of your company?" he drawled without bothering to stand or inviting them to sit down.

"Afternoon, Curtis. I want to talk to you about your friend Gerald Gaskill."

"I thought you might. We had a couple of your flatfoots around here this morning." Eric Curtis's eyes had travelled to Dorothy and were studying her with the same intensity as they had the day's runners and riders. She tried very hard not to squirm under his gaze. "I must say, old boy, your new assistant is a vast improvement on Sergeant Clark."

The inspector raised an eyebrow, but she was relieved when he didn't introduce her to Eric Curtis.

"Can you confirm that Gerald Gaskill was with you from eleven o'clock the night before last?" he asked instead.

"Yes, he arrived at about ten to eleven and didn't leave until the early hours. So, if you are looking for the man who killed his uncle, I'm afraid you will have to look elsewhere, old boy."

"You already know about his uncle?"

Curtis casually shrugged and leant back. "Good news travels fast, Derwent. Perhaps Gerry might be able to settle his bar bill now."

"Does he spend a lot of time here?"

"Ciro's is his second home."

"And he owes you money?"

"Me and half the bookmakers in the city. What can I say, Derwent? Gerry likes fast women and fast horses, not that he has much luck with either. Why don't you have a chat with Bessie? She spent most of the...how do you put it?...the night in question with Gerry. He finds her company far preferable to mine. The two of them are old friends."

He pointed over to the bar where a skinny young blonde woman, dressed in a crimson silk gown with matching gloves and wearing dark glasses was perched on a stool, sipping a cocktail.

"Does Bessie have a surname?"

"She does."

Inspector Derwent glared at him impatiently.

Curtis grinned. "Bessie Shelton," he replied, then turned his attention back to his newspaper. Dorothy and the inspector made their way over to the young woman and when they got closer, Dorothy could see her face was covered in a thick layer of makeup. From the way she was swaying on the bar stool, she suspected the cocktail wasn't the young woman's first drink of the day.

"Bessie Shelton?" enquired the inspector.

The woman twisted around in the stool but didn't remove her glasses. "Who wants to know?"

"My name is Inspector Derwent. I'm from Scotland Yard, and this is Miss Dorothy Peto from the Women Police Volunteers. We'd like to ask you a few questions about Mr Gerald Gaskill."

"What about him?" she asked, sounding wary.

"I understand he was here the night before last?" the inspector began.

"That's right. He's here most nights."

"We've been told he arrived shortly before eleven o'clock and didn't leave until half past two or three o'clock."

"That's right."

"He couldn't have slipped away for an hour or two perhaps?"

"No, he was with me the whole time and we left together and went to my place."

"You sound very sure."

"I am, Inspector. I charge by the hour. It's in my interest to keep track of when certain men arrive and when they leave."

She drained her glass and slammed it down on the bar. "Another martini, Tony."

"You're running up quite a tab, Bessie, and it's not even dark outside," replied the barman evenly.

"What's it to you? It'll get paid. Somebody always pays." She twisted around in her chair and flung out her arm dramatically towards him. "Your bar's a disgrace. That mirror is filthy. A bit of white vinegar, an old newspaper and some elbow grease, and it would come up a treat. It would gleam, I tell you."

The barman turned away shaking his head.

"See, you don't like it, do you? Someone telling you what to do. Then don't you be telling me."

Bessie's voice was growing louder and more high-pitched. Two of the girls on the dance floor looked over to them. The inspector tapped Dorothy gently on the shoulder.

"Time we were leaving I think, Miss Peto." Then raising his voice: "Thank you for your time, Bessie."

"Oh she's Miss Peto, but I'm just Bessie, am I? It's Miss Shelton to you. Miss Shelton."

Chapter Seven

WITH SOME RELIEF, Dorothy followed the inspector outside. As they stepped into the bright sunshine, Bessie's shouts were still ringing in their ears. Dorothy took a deep breath of the smoke-free air.

"She was rather argumentative."

The inspector nodded. "It was the drink talking."

"They do say you can judge a man by the company he keeps."

"Then I think we know everything we need to about Mr Gerald Gaskill. I apologise if you were offended by what you heard in there, Miss Peto."

"Not at all, Inspector, and you did warn me. I didn't like Curtis one jot, but I felt rather sad for Bessie. Why do you think she was wearing dark glasses indoors?"

"A silly affectation. Although if I were to spend any length of time in that establishment, I should probably wish to shield my eyes too."

The two of them strolled along in silence for a few moments.

"You're unusually quiet today. Is something bothering you, Miss Peto?" enquired the inspector.

"It wasn't just Paul Gaskill who died at the Battle of

Loos. I found out yesterday that George Sledmere was killed too."

Inspector Derwent stopped and turned towards her.

"I'm very sorry, Miss Peto. I know you were fond of him and that he was close to your family."

"Thank you, Inspector. We shall all miss him terribly and I suppose it has made me consider how horribly unfair life can be. Someone as good-natured and kind as George loses his life before he even turns twenty-five, yet an unpleasant man like Eric Curtis is still enjoying his. Paul Gaskill dies serving his country and a cad like Gerald may well become a very rich man."

The inspector shook his head. "You're quite correct, Miss Peto. Life isn't fair. Both young men died before their time. We can do nothing about Lord Sledmere or Paul Gaskill, but we can honour them by upholding the values of the country they died fighting for and bring Hector's killer to justice."

Dorothy knew he was right. She would serve the memory of George and Paul for that matter, not by moping and weeping, but by concentrating on investigating the death of the old man and ensuring that evil did not prosper. The two of them began walking again.

"Remembering what you said the other day, about motive and opportunity, it would seem from the information Mr Pearson and Mr Curtis gave us, that Gerald had a motive. He was in debt and lived beyond his means. Perhaps he thought killing his uncle and destroying the new will would solve his problems."

"True, he may have the motive, but if his friends at Ciro's are to be believed, not the opportunity. He also claims he did not know he was witnessing a will. Now he may be telling the truth; he may not. However, if he did know he had been disinherited, then it would have been in his interest for Hector to live in the hope that he may change his mind and put him or his wife back in the will. He may not have a high opinion of Mr Pearson, but could he know for sure there wasn't a second copy of the new will?"

Dorothy clicked her tongue impatiently. What he was saying made sense, but she didn't like it. She was sure Gerald was involved in Hector's death somehow, despite what Bessie and Curtis had told them.

"Did you check to see if Gerald's shoe matched the print you found in the mud?" she asked.

The inspector gave her a sidelong glance. "Yes, we did and no it didn't. His evening shoe had a smooth sole; the print we found in the garden had a deep, heavy tread, like a working man's boot. I know you dislike the man but you can't let that get in the way of the facts."

Before Dorothy could reply, the large figure of Sergeant Brook appeared around the corner.

"Sir; Miss Peto. We've found one of the missing candle-sticks. At a pawnbroker's on the King's Road. The owner said a man answering Duckworth's description brought it in. He's a regular client of theirs apparently."

"Now we know where he went before we arrived and why," said the inspector. "He wasn't composing himself, Miss Peto. He was feathering his nest and possibly getting rid of the murder weapon."

Dorothy bristled slightly. "Well, I admit that I may have been wrong about him being upset, but doesn't what Sergeant Brook has told us make it more likely he isn't the killer? If one of the candlesticks was the murder weapon, then surely he wouldn't risk doing anything to connect himself to it. These days it's common knowledge that the police are able to identify people by fingerprints they may have left behind."

"Desperate men do desperate things, Miss Peto, and from the betting slips we found under Duckworth's bed, I'd say Gerald Gaskill isn't the only suspect who owes money to bookmakers. As for whether the candlestick was used to kill Hector Gaskill, we won't know that for sure until Willerby has worked his magic."

"Taylor has taken it to him already, sir," said Sergeant Brook.

"Good. Then I think it's time I had another word with Mr Duckworth. Let's get to Cheyne Row before anyone tips him off. Good day, Miss Peto."

And with a quick tip of his hat, the inspector and his sergeant hurried away. Dorothy could only watch in frustration as they left her behind. The church bells of St Martin in the Fields began striking four o'clock and she realised in horror that she was due on patrol with Mary in less than an hour. It had been so long since she'd been out on patrol, she'd forgotten all about it.

She arrived back at the WPV offices on Little George Street, out of breath, and found Mary waiting impatiently for her.

"I'm sorry I'm late," she panted.

"About time, Dorothy! Come along. We have an important mission to attend to."

"Really? What?" asked Dorothy, suddenly brightening.

"There have been complaints about young boys jumping into the lake in Hyde Park, completely naked," explained Mary as she began marching down the street. Dorothy's heart sank.

"You can hardly blame them with this heat," she replied, wishing her colleague would slow down.

"That's no excuse for outraging public decency, Dorothy."

"How's Margaret?"

"Back at her desk. I told her she should have rested a little longer, but you know how she likes to be busy. It's probably a good idea that there's someone to keep an eye on Nina too." She gestured to the building behind them. "Where have you been anyway? It's not like you to be late."

"I took the telegram about Paul Gaskill to Scotland Yard and then to Mr Pearson the solicitor. He's a kind man and seems rather fond of Emily Gaskill, Hector's ward. The girl who married Gerald Gaskill."

"She was like a lamb to the slaughter."

"I met Gerald too."

"Poor you!"

"Mary, what did you mean about Hector Gaskill's servants being treated badly and the maids leaving?"

"He got through quite a few of them and I firmly believe the blame lay with his nephew."

"Why?"

"Let's just say Gerald thinks the maids are there to do more than clean and tidy for him. If it wasn't maids, it was chorus girls from the music hall. Hector thought marriage might calm him down and poor Emily, well she wasn't exactly inundated with alternative offers. Hector said he didn't want her ending up an old maid. As I said, he was a dreadful man, and I wouldn't be surprised if his nephew wasn't responsible for his death."

"Gerald has an alibi for the time he died," explained Dorothy.

"Well, I hope Inspector Derwent isn't taking it on face value. I wouldn't believe a word Gerald Gaskill says."

It was rare for Dorothy to find herself agreeing with Mary these days. She thought she'd find out where she stood on another subject Dorothy had been thinking about.

"Nina was telling me about how many forces are wanting to employ our members," she began tentatively but Mary immediately gave a snort of derision.

"I think it's a ridiculous idea—whatever the National Council of Women and Nina say. A dog can't serve two masters. Either they are part of our organisation or they aren't."

Dorothy wasn't particularly offended by Mary comparing her and the other volunteers to dogs, but she thought she was wrong. One of her aunts sent her Labrador to stay with Dorothy's parents each year while she spent a few months in Italy. The Labrador was devoted to her aunt, but he was quite happy to trot at her father's heel while she was away. Dorothy was about to argue this point, but they had arrived at the gates of Hyde Park and Mary suddenly began sprinting across the grass.

"There they are, the little hooligans. Come along, Dorothy. If we're quick, we'll catch them," she yelled as she headed towards a group of small naked boys by the lake, and Dorothy could do nothing but chase after her.

THE NEXT MORNING, London's Indian summer showed no sign of ending. The air was hot and heavy. Dorothy was sitting at her desk in the anti-office typing up a list of the latest recruits. She had opened all the windows and doors hoping, in vain, for a cooling breeze. Nina and Margaret were both at their desks too but despite the outside heat, the atmosphere in their office was rather chilly. This morning Nina's head was buried in a newspaper, while Margaret methodically added her signature to the large pile of cheques stacked in front of her. From the very start it had been Margaret and her vast fortune bankrolling the WPV.

"Oh I don't believe it!" exclaimed Nina suddenly. Margaret looked up wearily. Dorothy knew she was still feeling rather weak from her bout of food poisoning, but over the last few weeks, it had also become obvious that she was getting rather bored of her deputy's dramatic outbursts.

"What's wrong now, Nina?" she asked.

"Dora!" Nina replied slapping the newspaper down loudly. Margaret's forehead creased into a frown.

"Who's she? One of the new recruits?"

"No, D. O. R. A. Dora! Honestly, do you never read the newspapers, Margaret? It stands for the Defence of the Realm Act."

"Oh I see, all that nonsense about not flying kites or buying binoculars," tutted Margaret, returning to the cheques waiting to be signed.

"It just got a lot more serious. Listen to this."

Nina picked up the newspaper again and began to read in her loud clear voice.

"Yesterday, a novel court martial was held at Cardiff, when five women of a certain class were tried, under the Defence of the Realm Act, for being out of doors between the hours of seven pm and eight am. An order had been issued by Colonel East, commanding the Severn Defences, closing public houses in the city to women customers between the hours of seven pm and six am. Accused women who pleaded guilty have been arrested in various parts of the city during prohibited hours. It was stated that officers who served notices upon the women read and explained the order to those who were themselves unable to read. The magistrate pointed out that the women were liable to punishment not exceeding three months' imprisonment. It was intimated that the sentences of the court would be submitted to the colonel in due course—the women, meanwhile, being detained in custody."

Nina threw the newspaper to the floor in disgust. "They are subjecting women to a curfew. All women. Aren't you outraged?" she demanded.

Margaret shook her head as she calmly slid the last of the cheques into an envelope. "Not particularly. I don't think a curfew will work. I imagine men will just visit these women in their homes and carry on their activities there instead."

Nina leapt to her feet, her chair scraping across the floor as she did so.

Margaret's face grew solemn. "These theatrics really are

becoming quite tiresome, Nina," she complained, almost under her breath.

Nina ignored her and began pacing up and down. Dorothy watched the two of them through her door with a growing sense of foreboding. She knew that look on Nina's face. It was her 'spoiling for a fight' look. The question was, would Margaret do anything to avoid an argument as was usually the case, or would Nina push her too far?

"I simply can't understand why you don't share my sense of outrage, Margaret. You are as familiar as I am with hearing examples of how women are treated unjustly under the laws of our land. Dorothy and I, and other members of the Women's Freedom League, complied a vast collection before the outbreak of war." In the outer office, Dorothy ducked her head down, not wanting to be drawn into the argument as Nina railed on. "When we formed the WPV, I never imagined anyone would ask me to be complicit in carrying these injustices out. Yet, your attitude leads me to believe you would be prepared to allow the WPV to enforce these curfews."

"Yes, I would. As I have said countless times before, if we want to be taken seriously, we must do everything that is asked of us," explained Margaret calmly, placing an elastic band around the bundle of envelopes. Nina stopped abruptly in front of her desk and cleared her throat.

"If that is how you truly feel, then I think you should reconsider your position as commandant of the Women Police Volunteers," she declared.

Dorothy held her breath and watched.

Margaret rose to her feet and looked Nina in the eye.

"And I think we should let our members decide the course of action our organisation should take."

Nina placed her hands on her hips and nodded her head in agreement. "Then I'll call a meeting of our members and we will put it to them."

"No," replied Margaret, "as commandant, I shall call the meeting."

Without another word, Nina turned on her heel and stalked out of the office, ignoring Dorothy as she passed by and slamming the door behind her, causing the windows to shake. Margaret watched her go, then calmly returned to her seat.

Dorothy was torn. In essence, she agreed with Nina. The Defence of the Realm Act was yet again blaming women for the rise in prostitution and for the inevitable increase in sexually transmitted diseases. However, she understood Margaret's point too. She, Mary, Nina and Dorothy had all promised Sir Edward Henry, the head of Scotland Yard, that they would uphold all laws, when he gave them permission to form the WPV. These new laws would be enforced whatever they thought and surely it was better that the WPV were involved rather than leave it to the overstretched regular police or the army, as had happened in Cardiff.

She glanced into the office. Margaret was now busy sharing shortbread biscuits with her three dogs who had remained remarkably quiet throughout their mistress's confrontation. Dorothy decided she should go after Nina and convince her to make peace with Margaret, before Mary heard about the meeting. She was sure to encourage the idea, knowing that if Nina lost the vote, she was bound to resign.

Dorothy couldn't bear that thought. Quietly, she picked up her hat and tiptoed out the office and down the stairs.

Out in the street there was no sign of Nina. Dorothy started to head down Whitehall towards the Strand. The Women's Freedom League's offices were located just off there on Robert Street. Nina may have gone there looking for old comrades to give her support. However, Dorothy had only taken a few steps when she heard someone call out.

"Miss Peto! Miss Peto!" She turned at the sound of her name and saw a young woman standing in a doorway, a shawl covering her head despite the heat.

"Connie? Is that you? What are you doing here?" she asked in surprise.

The young woman stepped forward. She looked even paler and more worried than when Dorothy had last seen her. "I've been waiting for you, miss. I hoped you might come out. I'm sorry to bother you, but I didn't know where else to go and you were so kind to me the other day."

"What's the matter? Has something happened?"

The young woman's lip began tremble. "Yes, miss. They have arrested Jack."

"Who?"

"Jack Hurst. He and I, well we've been stepping out together. He works for his uncle who has a gardening business. He cuts the grass once a week and tends the flower beds for Mr Gaskill—or at least he did. They think he killed Mr Gaskill and stole a candlestick and the watch. But I know he didn't do it. He would never do such a wicked thing."

A tear trickled down her face. Dorothy patted her arm, but she was a little confused. The last time she'd seen the inspector he'd been hot on the heels of Duckworth. There had been no mention of the gardener's boy.

At that moment, she saw Margaret and her dogs coming down the steps of the WPV offices, no doubt off to the post office with the pile of envelopes she was carrying.

"Look, Connie, why don't you come into our offices. The place is empty now and you can tell me everything."

The young maid nodded nervously and followed Dorothy inside. Dorothy settled her down on to one of the sofas in the main room and, despite her protests, made them both a cup of tea.

"Now, Connie," she began, sitting down opposite her, "why on earth do the police think your young man Jack killed Mr Gaskill?"

"It's all my fault, miss. You see, I spent the night with him. The whole night." She put her cup down and covered her face with her hands. "Oh I know it's a sin, but we want to be married. It's just we've been saving up and then war broke out and Jack wanted to do his duty. He's enlisted in the army. He would have joined up sooner, but his uncle has been ill, and he needed to keep the business going. But his training was due to begin tomorrow, and it was our last chance to be together."

Connie was gabbling away so quickly and her voice was so muffled that Dorothy was struggling to keep up. She handed the young woman her handkerchief.

"So, the two of you spent the whole of Saturday night together?"

"Yes, I just pretended to go to bed. I waited until I could hear Mrs Platt snoring, then I crept back downstairs. Mr

Duckworth was in his pantry but, well, you see he…"

"Had been drinking and was asleep too."

"Yes, miss. He often falls asleep there. It's true he enjoys a drink but only after he's finished his duties. He wouldn't drink when he was working. I slipped out of the kitchen door and then went through the garden gate where Jack was waiting for me. We'd planned it, you see. We went to his uncle's house. He was away for the night. He'd gone down to Brighton to see a friend of his." She wiped her eyes and had stopped weeping, but her face was becoming redder by the second. "It was our only chance, and we weren't to know poor Mr Gaskill would be killed on the same night. But then the police found out I hadn't slept in my bed and accused me of lying. I didn't know what to say. I couldn't tell anyone where I had been. I'd lose my job. Mr Gaskill always insisted his servants should be of good moral character. But I don't even know who I work for now poor Mr Paul has gone too." Tears began to roll down her face again.

"I'm sorry, Connie, but I still don't understand why Inspector Derwent has arrested Jack?"

"It was the footprint that did it for him, miss. The one they found by the birdbath. It was Jack's. The police called at his house to check. Then they found his shirt with the bloodstain, but when they asked him about it, he wouldn't tell them anything. He was protecting me."

"Hold on, whose blood was it and how did it get on his shirt?"

"Mr Gaskill's, miss. We left Jack's uncle's house before dawn and he walked me back to Cheyne Row. We stopped by the birdbath so he could give me a kiss goodbye and that's when we saw him. Mr Gaskill lying by the bird table. We both ran over. Jack touched his face and we knew he was dead, but Jack got a bit of the poor man's blood on his sleeve. That man who was with you in the library, he'll know it was blood won't he? He'll be able to prove it. Mr Duckworth said that's what he was looking for." Her voice was rising in panic again as she talked about Willerby. "I know we should have told someone there and then, but he was dead, and we'd have both got into trouble. Now the police have found out anyway and taken Jack away. The thing is, miss, he won't be able to defend himself. They'll question him, but I know Jack won't tell the police I was with him. He'll protect me. I want to help him, but I don't know what to do or where he is."

"Please calm down, Connie. We'll find out where Jack is, but we will need to convince the inspector that he wasn't involved in Mr Gaskill's death at all," said Dorothy. Her first instinct was to feel sympathy for the maid, and she certainly sounded convincing, but she had to remind herself that Connie had lied to her before. "Now, when you returned to Cheyne Row, did you hear or see anything unusual?"

"No, miss. We didn't see another soul. There was some distant whistling, but I think that was just the milkman delivering to the front of the house."

"What time did you return home?"

"It was a little before half past five. The longcase clock in the hall was striking as I arrived back in the kitchen. It was almost time for Mrs Platt to get up so I thought I'd get on and light the stove."

"And Jack went straight back to his uncle's house.

There's nothing else you need to tell me about him?"

Connie looked down at her hands and began twisting the handkerchief around her fingers.

"There is one thing, miss. When we went to check on Mr Gaskill, we could see his watch was hanging out of his pocket. It was one of them old-fashioned ones on a chain. Jack picked it up. The face had been smashed and the hands had stopped at half past three. Then I remembered I'd read that the police could find fingerprints on things these days, so I told Jack to get rid of the watch in case they found his prints. He took it and told me he would throw it in the river."

Dorothy tried not to groan. If Connie's young man really was innocent, then he certainly hadn't made things easy for himself.

"Are you sure he wouldn't have taken it and tried to sell it? Even if the watch was broken the gold chain might have been worth something?"

Connie looked shocked. "Oh no, miss, Jack wouldn't do that. Oh what am I going to do?" she wailed.

Dorothy sighed. "There's nothing for it. I think you'll have to go to Scotland Yard and explain everything to Inspector Derwent," she began, but Connie started shaking her head in horror.

"But Mr Duckworth is sure to find out. I'll be sacked on the spot. My reputation will be done for. I'll never get another position. I'll be out on the streets. And what if they don't believe me? What if they think I'm just saying it to save Jack?"

Dorothy could see her point. The cynical inspector already thought Connie was a liar and she wouldn't be at all surprised if he didn't believe the poor young woman or even charged her with withholding evidence or some such crime. Dorothy, however, did believe her. She sounded truly sincere and although Dorothy may never have been in love herself, the romantic in her could imagine the desperation of two young people who were prepared to risk everything to be together.

"Look," she said standing up. "How would it be if I go to see Inspector Derwent and explain everything, including why you didn't tell him the truth? I can't promise it will do any good or that he won't want to speak to you himself, but it would be a start."

Connie looked like she was going to faint with relief as she staggered to her feet and clutched Dorothy's hands.

"Oh, miss, would you really? The inspector is bound to listen to you. You'll know what to say. I'd be ever so grateful, and I know Jack will be too."

The two of them left the offices and parted company with Connie still thanking Dorothy profusely. Connie headed back to Chelsea while Dorothy set off down White-hall once more, hoping that Connie's faith in her wasn't misplaced.

Chapter Eight

DOROTHY FOUND THE inspector in the incident room they had set up for the investigation into Hector Gaskill's death. He was standing in front of a desk reading from a sheet of paper while Sergeant Clark was bashing slowly away at a typewriter and Sergeant Taylor was speaking on the telephone.

"Hello, gentlemen," she said brightly as she entered the room. Clark and Taylor nodded politely. Neither of them looked particularly surprised to see her there.

"Good afternoon, Miss Peto. How can I help you?" asked the inspector putting the sheet of paper down.

"Actually, I think I might be able to help you, Inspector. I'm afraid you've got the wrong man. Jack Hurst didn't steal anything, and he didn't kill Mr Gaskill."

Inspector Derwent raised an eyebrow. "Is that so?"

"Yes, in fact I was rather surprised to hear that you had arrested him. I thought you would be questioning Mr Duckworth after you found the missing candlestick."

"We would be, had we been able to find him."

"He's disappeared? Surely that's a sign of his guilt."

"Perhaps or perhaps he's simply in a drunken stupor in one of the city's hostelries. We have Sergeant Brook watching the house on Cheyne Row, waiting for him to return, if he ever does. As for Hurst, he had access to the house, plenty of opportunities to case the place, and a man matching his description was seen loitering by the garden gate on the evening in question. Then there is the footprint that places him there and a stain on his shirtsleeve that may well be blood. I've also just discovered he has a criminal record."

"Really?" Dorothy asked in surprise. She peered at the sheet of paper lying on the desk in front of him and although it was upside down, managed to read what it said. For once, it was her turn to raise an eyebrow at the inspector.

"It's a bit of a stretch from scrumping apples four years ago to murder, don't you think, Inspector?" she queried demurely.

Sitting in his corner, Sergeant Clark was suddenly struck by a coughing fit and, to Dorothy's amusement, the inspector began straightening his tie as he cleared his throat.

"That may be the case, Miss Peto, but it doesn't change the fact that Hurst has no alibi."

"Ah, but he does. However, it's rather a delicate matter."

"Delicate how?"

"He was with a young woman all night."

The two other detectives looked up.

"What young woman?" asked the inspector.

"Connie the parlour maid. You'll recall her own bed hadn't been slept in." Was it her imagination, or had his face reddened slightly?

"Hurst said he was alone all night."

"I think he's trying to protect Connie's reputation. It's really rather gallant of him. Hardly the behaviour of a murderer. By the way, that stain definitely is blood. He touched Mr Gaskill's face to check for any sign of life."

"May I ask how you know all this, Miss Peto?"

"Connie came to see me. She was terribly upset about Jack, but also terribly worried that you wouldn't believe her."

The inspector folded his arms and grunted. "As well she should be after the merry dance she has led us on. She'll be lucky if I don't charge her with withholding evidence or obstruction."

"I quite understand, Inspector, but surely the important thing is she's telling the truth now. She told me that she waited until she could hear Mrs Platt snoring, snuck past Mr Duckworth who had been drinking—the brandy probably— and was dozing in the pantry. Then she met Jack who was waiting for her by the gate. When they returned to the house a little before half past five, Mr Gaskill was already dead in the garden. Jack touched his face and also picked up his watch. The face was smashed, and the hands were stuck at the half past three position. Connie was worried about the police finding his fingerprints, so Jack said he would throw it in the river, and they didn't see or hear anyone else, except possibly a whistling milkman. Yes, I think that's everything," she ended a little breathlessly.

The inspector stared at her for a second, his expression unreadable. "Clark, get down to the cells and speak to Hurst again. Tell him we know about Connie and see if this alibi stacks up. Find out exactly what happened to Gaskill's watch. If this business about the river is true, get uniform to start dredging. There's a chance it might still be there."

"Yes, sir," replied the older sergeant eagerly, leaving the

typewriter behind and hurrying out of the door.

At the same time, Taylor put down the telephone receiver. "That was Brook, sir. Duckworth is back."

"Good, I'll get down to Chelsea, before he disappears again."

"Might I be allowed to sit in on the interview with Jack?" Dorothy asked hopefully, but the inspector gave a firm shake of his head as he reached for his hat and coat.

"No doubt you will think me old-fashioned Miss Peto, but I don't think that is a suitable discussion for you to witness, and I dare say Sergeant Clark will have more luck talking to Hurst man to man."

Dorothy's shoulders sagged. She had hoped to be able to reassure Jack that Connie wanted him to tell the truth.

"Instead, perhaps you would be kind enough to accompany me to Cheyne Row."

"You want me to be there when you speak to Mr Duckworth?" she asked unable to keep the delight out of her voice.

"More specifically when I speak to Connie. If what she told you is indeed true, we might have more luck getting her to repeat it in front of you."

"Don't you believe her story?"

"She may be telling the truth, but I'd like to hear it from her myself. She seems to be a rather bright young woman. It was Connie who drew our attention to the missing candlesticks and how many housemaids are aware of the police using fingerprints?" Dorothy was about to reply that she thought any young woman was capable of reading newspaper reports on police investigations, whatever her situation in life, but the inspector was still talking as he strode towards the door. "For all we know, she and Hurst could be in on some kind of conspiracy with Duckworth and are trying to deflect our attention," he continued.

"She seemed very genuine when she spoke to me. I think she and Jack are just a young couple in love who were in the wrong place at the wrong time."

The inspector snorted. "It sounds like the plot from a book Mr Lawrence might have written."

"Oh, DH Lawrence is such a wonderful writer. I have huge admiration for his work."

His mouth twisted into a wry smile. "I thought you might."

Dorothy travelled with the inspector and Sergeant Taylor to Chelsea in a police motorcar. Inspector Derwent instructed the driver to stop at the end of Cheyne Row and wait as the three of them stepped out.

"Brook will still be watching the front door. You go to the rear in case he makes a run for it through the garden," the inspector instructed Sergeant Taylor. Then he and Dorothy approached the front door of number twelve and rang the bell. Duckworth opened the door to them and if he was worried about their visit, he didn't show it.

"Mr Duckworth, may we speak with you?"

"Certainly, Inspector Derwent, please step inside. If you would care to follow me into the library?"

"One of my sergeants called yesterday afternoon, hoping to speak to you, but you were not here."

"That's correct, sir. I was visiting my sister. It was my half-day off. We are each of us entitled to one. Today is

Connie's. Mrs Platt's is tomorrow."

Dorothy glanced over to Inspector Derwent. It looked like he wouldn't be able to talk to the maid after all, but he didn't react to the news.

"I'd like to talk to you about the morning Mr Gaskill's body was discovered. I understand you went for a walk shortly before my men and I arrived. Can you tell me where you went?"

"Just for a stroll, sir. Down to the river. I was shocked by what had happened to Mr Gaskill. I needed some fresh air to try to clear my head."

"So, you didn't pay a visit to an establishment on the King's Road?"

The butler nervously licked his lips. "No, I don't believe I did, sir."

"That's very odd, Mr Duckworth, because a man answering your description took a single silver candlestick to a pawnbroker there. We believe it is one of the missing candlesticks from this very room. Our expert has been able to confirm that the shape and weight of the item would fit the weapon used to strike and kill Mr Gaskill. Perhaps you would like to reconsider your previous answer and tell us where the other candlestick is."

Duckworth had grown very pale and his hands were beginning to tremble.

"All right, I admit I took one of the candlesticks from here, but I don't know what happened to the other one. When Miss Damer Dawson arrived and we found out Mr Gaskill was dead, I was shocked and upset but not just by his death. You see I actually did overhear him talking to Mr

Pearson, the solicitor. I knew he'd changed his will and hadn't left me anything."

"So, you were angry with Mr Gaskill?" asked the inspector.

Duckworth's eyes flashed. "Of course I was angry with him. I'd served him for twenty years. He wasn't an easy man to work for and he didn't pay as well as I could have got elsewhere, but he told me I would be provided for in my old age. He promised."

His voice was beginning to rise and there was a hint of his native Kent accent slipping out. Dorothy could see his eyes kept flicking to the decanters on the sideboard.

"Did you confront him? Quarrel with him? Lose your temper?"

"No! He didn't know that I knew." He paused. "I was in the dining room laying the table for supper and happened to overhear the two gentlemen discussing the matter."

Dorothy glanced over to the heavy door that led into the dining room. She very much doubted you would be able to hear anything through it unless you had your ear pressed up against it. The inspector's expression was equally sceptical.

"Did you also happen to hear the reason Mr Gaskill gave for wanting to change his will?"

"No. I only heard the master dictating to Mr Pearson. He said everything was to go to Mr Paul."

"I suggest he was leaving you out of the will because he had discovered you had been stealing from him. The pawnbroker told my officer that you regularly visit them."

Glistening beads of sweat were appearing on the butler's forehead and as he reached in his pocket for his handkerchief, Dorothy noticed his hand was trembling.

"No, he couldn't have done," he stammered. "I only took in a few bits and pieces the master wouldn't notice. A silver spoon or an old silk handkerchief. I planned to get them all back just as soon as my luck changed. Besides, I wasn't the only one who didn't want him to change his will. Mrs Platt was due to lose her annuity too."

"I doubt she could have overheard him. Did you speak to Mrs Platt about the will?" asked the inspector.

Both Duckworth's hands were shaking now. "No, but she could have found out herself and she'd rowed with him the day he died."

"Rowed? What about?"

"She wanted a pay rise. He wouldn't give it to her. Then he threatened her with the sack. He said she was too deaf to work for him, said she couldn't hear the bell properly when he rang and that his dinner was cold." His voice was becoming louder and more desperate with every word.

"Is that true?" asked Dorothy.

The butler shrugged. "It's true she can't hear so well, but Connie is usually with her—she lets her know when the bell rings."

"I think we need to speak to Mrs Platt again. Fetch her please, Mr Duckworth."

"I'm sorry, sir. I can't. She's also out. She's gone to the butcher's and the fishmonger's, I believe."

"I would have thought Mrs Platt would have arranged a weekly delivery from them," said Dorothy. At that moment, there was a loud bump above their heads. Dorothy looked at the inspector, then they both looked at Duckworth.

"If Mrs Platt and Connie are both out, who is upstairs?" asked the inspector.

"That would be Mr Gerald, sir." The butler cleared his throat. "He has decided to move in. Into Mr Paul's room in fact." Despite all his faults, Dorothy could see that Duckworth was clearly uncomfortable with this arrangement and she didn't blame him. He turned to address at her. "You are quite correct, Miss Peto. Usually the tradesmen deliver every Friday, but Mr Gerald is holding a small party this evening and requested some items that required Mrs Platt to make a special shopping trip."

"I see," replied the inspector. He stood up and waved to Sergeant Taylor, who was standing like a sentry at the end of the garden.

"David Duckworth, I am arresting you for the theft of a silver candlestick…" he began.

The butler didn't reply, but simply nodded as he rose unsteadily to his feet. Dorothy couldn't help but pity him. She let Sergeant Taylor in through the garden door, who promptly placed the butler in handcuffs.

"Take him to the car," instructed the inspector.

"Please, sir, may I be allowed to leave through the garden?" asked the butler in a quiet voice. "I've been butler to this house for twenty years. People, I mean, I have a certain standing amongst our neighbours."

The inspector gave the sergeant a brisk nod.

"Shall we wait for you, sir?" asked Taylor.

"No, Sergeant. Take him back to the Yard and charge him. I'll join you later."

Dorothy opened the door for the two men and watched

as Taylor led the butler away, his head low with shame.

"Shall we, Miss Peto?" enquired Inspector Derwent. She followed him out into the hall and they were greeted by the sound of cheerful whistling and quick heavy footsteps coming down the stairs. They looked up to see Gerald. He was carrying a box of cigars in one hand and a silver-topped cane in the other. He came to a halt when he saw them.

"Ah, Inspector Derwent and the charming Miss Peto. What brings you here?"

"Our ongoing investigation into the murder of your uncle, Mr Gaskill. May I ask you the same question?"

"It seemed a shame to let Havana's finest go to waste. Uncle Hector only smoked one at Christmas and on the king's birthday and my own cane is looking a little worn. Besides, after the news about Paul, it must only be a matter of time until this place and everything in it comes to me."

"Indeed. I understand you have moved in."

Gerald looked furious for a second, then quickly switched on his easy smile. "I thought it would be a good idea to keep an eye on my inheritance, as old Pearson seems to be dragging his heels. Keeps droning on about applying for probate and so forth. You know how lawyers are."

"Will Mrs Gaskill be joining you here, Mr Gaskill?"

"No, I saw no need to disturb Emily. She isn't too fond of change and seems quite happy where she is."

"So she won't be attending your party this evening?"

Gerald's easy smile tightened a little. "Hardly a party, Inspector. More a small gathering to commemorate the lives of dear Uncle Hector and Paul. Both taken too soon and all that."

"I see, sir. Well, I'm sorry to inform you that you shall have to manage without a butler. Mr Duckworth is under arrest for the theft of a silver candlestick from this house."

Gerald seemed to find this information amusing rather than shocking.

"Well, well, well. I didn't know old Duckworth had it in him. Not to fret, Inspector. I'm sure between them Connie and Mrs Platt will manage superbly and, who knows, under your expert interrogation you might even find that it was Duckworth who did for poor old Uncle Hector. Isn't that what happens in all the murder mystery novels? The butler did it!"

Dorothy and Inspector Derwent stepped out on to the street with Gerald's laughter echoing behind them.

"Such a dreadful man! Imagine entertaining while his uncle lies in the city morgue. Is he allowed to be in the house?" asked Dorothy.

The inspector shrugged. "Between him and Duckworth, I'm surprised the place hasn't been completely ransacked. There might not be much left for Pearson to value for probate."

"And he was still in evening dress. Does he never go home, even to change?"

"Why don't we pay his wife a visit and ask her?" suggested the inspector.

"Emily? Do you have her address?"

"It would be rather foolish to suggest visiting her if I did not, Miss Peto."

Dorothy didn't rise to the bait, instead she fell into step next to him as he strode along, his stick tapping the pavement rhythmically once more.

"I thought Duckworth was telling the truth. I think he has an awful lot of problems. I wouldn't be surprised if he owed people money. You said you'd found lots of betting slips and then there's the drink. I think he thought nobody would notice the missing candlestick in all the hubbub surrounding Hector's death."

"You seem to find it far easier to believe Hector Gaskill's servants than his nephew. Despite Gerald having an alibi."

"I hardly think those providing his alibi could be called trustworthy," muttered Dorothy.

"Perhaps not, but that would be up to a jury to decide."

"Doctor Stirk did say that due to the warm weather it was difficult to give an accurate time of death. Even if Bessie is telling the truth, there may have been time for him to return to his uncle's house."

"Yet, according to what Connie told you about the watch being smashed at half past three, we can safely assume Hector was not killed after that time."

Dorothy's face fell in disappointment.

"Oh yes, I forgot about that."

"Or chose not to remember. Besides, even without the watch, we have asked the cab drivers who were working in the area that night. One of them confirmed he took a man from Cheyne Row to Ciro's at around eleven o'clock, but none of them took a fare to Chelsea from there. Ciro's is at least an hour away on foot. If Gerald had tried to walk there, it would have taken too long."

Dorothy sighed quietly. It seemed she couldn't convince him that Gerald was their man. They walked on in silence over the bridge.

"Have you met Emily before?" she asked.

"No. By all accounts, she is a meek, God-fearing woman, who was on good terms with Hector. Faced with all the other suspects I have, talking to her hasn't been a priority."

"I'm not sure I agree. If someone had married me off to Gerald Gaskill, I would want to kill them," she replied.

The inspector's lips twitched. "Besides, if she is anything like the other females associated with this case, I thought it might be prudent to wait until there was an opportunity for you to accompany me."

Dorothy couldn't stop herself smiling. He had wanted her to be with him when he interviewed someone. That must mean he considered her to be of some value. She must be doing something right.

Chapter Nine

AFTER THEY HAD crossed Albert Bridge, they turned on to Prince of Wales Drive. The road overlooked Battersea Park. Dorothy grinned to herself as she spotted several young boys running around the boating lake wearing only their underpants. Mary would not be pleased. The inspector raised his walking stick and pointed to a red-brick mansion block.

"The Gaskills have a flat on the fourth floor," he explained.

"It looks rather smart," commented Dorothy.

The inspector nodded. "It does, but I dare say to a man like Gerald, not as smart as he would like. I imagine a Chelsea townhouse trumps a flat in Battersea."

They were about to cross the road, when the inspector placed a hand on her shoulder and nodded towards the entrance of the mansion block. The door had swung open and Arnold Pearson came hurrying out, his leather document case under his arm. They watched as he hailed a cab and drove off in the opposite direction.

"He told me he was going to visit Emily yesterday too. They must see an awful lot of each other," said Dorothy.

"So it would seem," agreed the inspector.

They walked into the foyer and stepped into the lift. Dorothy couldn't help feeling a little envious as they glided up to the fourth floor. If only her block of flats in Bloomsbury had one of these contraptions, it would certainly be better than carry bags full of groceries up three flights of stairs.

Inspector Derwent pressed the doorbell of flat number sixteen and a few seconds later, it was opened by a young woman, whom Dorothy recognised from the photograph in Arnold Pearson's office. She was dressed in black and wore no jewellery except for a plain gold wedding band and a small gold crucifix around her neck. Her hair was scraped back into a bun and perched on her head was a small black hat. The hat's veil covered her face, but it was still possible to see the deep purple colour running diagonally from the centre of her forehead across the right-hand side of her face.

"Mrs Gaskill?" enquired the inspector.

"Yes, I am Emily Gaskill," she replied in a quavering voice.

"My name is Inspector Derwent and this is Miss Peto from the Women Police Volunteers." Emily adjusted the veil slightly as she peered closely at the inspector's warrant card. "May we come in and speak with you regarding the death of Hector Gaskill?"

"Yes, of course, Inspector." She moved back, and Dorothy and the inspector stepped into the hallway. "This is such a terrible business. First Uncle Hector and then poor Paul. I've been praying for their souls since I heard the news. Such a terrible business," she repeated as she led them into a tidy, but sparsely furnished sitting room. "Please do take a seat.

May I offer you some tea?"

"No thank you, Mrs Gaskill," replied the inspector and Dorothy shook her head too.

"When did you last see Mr Gaskill?" asked the inspector as he lowered himself into one of the armchairs while Dorothy perched next to Emily on the chaise longue.

"Last Sunday. I had lunch with him after church."

"Did he mention that he was considering changing his will?"

"No, but then he never discussed such matters with me."

"Was your husband with you?"

"No, it was just the two of us. We always had lunch together on Sunday."

"Which church do you attend?"

"Chelsea Old Church on Cheyne Walk. I play the organ there every evensong as well as on Sundays."

"When did you last see your husband?"

Emily paused. "Not for…goodness it must be ten days now. Gerald is very rarely here, Inspector."

"Would it surprise you to learn that he has moved into twelve Cheyne Row?"

Emily looked thoughtful for a moment, then shook her head. "No. Not really. I thought he must have come home to collect his things, but I didn't know where he'd gone. I hardly ever know where he is."

"He came home to collect his things, but just now you said you hadn't seen him for ten days."

"Forgive me, Inspector. What I meant to say is, I could smell cigar smoke when I returned from church. Gerald is the only person I know who smokes cigars and the only other person with a front door key, so I assumed… I'm not certain though, as I haven't looked in Gerald's room. He doesn't like me to go into his room. We have separate rooms you see."

Dorothy could see the poor woman was becoming more and more flustered.

"Inspector, perhaps you would like to look at Mr Gaskill's room while I stay here with Mrs Gaskill," she suggested, giving him a meaningful look. He frowned at first then gave a brisk nod and left the room.

"Thank you," whispered Emily. "I do want to answer the inspector's questions, but…well it's rather embarrassing. You see, while it is true Gerald and I were married almost a year ago, he and I have never lived together as man and wife."

Now it was Dorothy's turn to frown. "I'm not sure I understand."

"We have always had separate rooms, separate beds. While that may not be so very unusual, I hear other couples have similar arrangements, but in their case—how should I put this?—there are at least occasional visits. That's not so in our case."

"Never?"

Emily shook her head. Dorothy hated to press the point, but it was important she was clear if she had to report this conversation back to the inspector.

"You mean after your wedding night…"

Emily held up her hand to interrupt her. "I spent our wedding night alone in a hotel in Torquay. The establishment had a casino. Gerald spent the night there. He told me before he went down that I should not wait for him. His exact words were: 'I have no intention of mounting a dog like you tonight or any other night. I shan't risk any child of mine bearing your devil's mark.'"

"What a truly rotten thing to say!" exclaimed Dorothy, outraged.

"He was drunk. He's often drunk. He only went through with the wedding because Uncle Hector agreed to pay off his gambling debts, but although his words stung rather, I must admit I was relieved. Not having a mother or another woman I could speak to, I had rather been dreading what might have occurred."

"Then why did you agree to go through with the wedding?"

"It was what Uncle Hector wanted. He'd been so good to me since Daddy died. I felt it would be a sin not to obey him." She paused and adjusted her veil. "Miss Peto, I confess there may also have been a little vanity on my part. I thought if I was a married woman, people would be less likely to pity me."

Dorothy gently patted her hand. She felt full of sympathy for the other woman.

"If the marriage…well, if it hasn't been consummated, doesn't that mean you could divorce Gerald?"

Emily recoiled in horror. "Oh, Miss Peto, I could never do that. Divorce is a sin in the eyes of God. 'What therefore God hath joined together, let not man put asunder'," she quoted, her hand instinctively reaching for the crucifix hanging around her neck.

"But aren't you lonely? Perhaps you could find happiness with someone else."

"The Lord never gives us more than we can bear. Really, Miss Peto, I have a very good life. I have the church and good friends like dear Arnold."

"Mr Pearson does seem very fond of you."

"He is a terribly kind man. I told him he should be called Peter—he's my rock as Peter was to Jesus."

Heavy footsteps and the tapping of a cane told Dorothy that the inspector had finished his examination of Gerald's room. He coughed loudly before entering the room.

"Thank you, Mrs Gaskill. Everything appears to be in order." He shot Dorothy an enquiring glance. She rose to her feet.

"Yes, thank you very much for your time," she said.

Emily smiled politely. "I shall pray for you both and ask the good Lord to guide you as you bring poor Uncle Hector's killer to justice," she said as she showed them out.

"Did you find anything of interest in Gerald's room?" asked Dorothy as the lift carried them down to the ground floor.

"No. It didn't look like anyone had slept in there recently and there was no sign of any personal effects. I checked the bathroom too. There was only one toothbrush and no shaving equipment. I think Emily was right. Gerald packed up his things while she was at church. It seems a very peculiar marriage."

"I don't think you can truly describe their relationship as a marriage. While you were out of the room, Emily confided in me that their union has never been consummated."

The inspector grunted. "Then she could be granted a divorce and be rid of him."

"That was precisely what I said, but she was horrified by the very idea."

They stepped out into the street and began their walk back to Chelsea.

"Did she mention Arnold Pearson?"

"She called him her rock, but she didn't tell me that he had visited her just before we arrived. Should I have asked?"

"No. Sometimes it's more interesting to see what information a suspect is willing to volunteer themselves and what they choose to conceal."

"Do you consider Emily to be a suspect?" she asked. To her mind, it didn't look like the young woman had the strength to lift a candlestick, let alone deliver a fatal blow.

The inspector shrugged.

"Oh, I do hope Mr Pearson isn't involved. He seems so nice," Dorothy said.

"Unlike Gerald the rogue. Unfortunately, in my experience, murders are often rather good at pretending to be something they are not."

"Then Gerald should be trying harder to be a decent human being," tutted Dorothy.

They made their way back across Albert Bridge. As they got closer to Chelsea, they could see a swarm of dark blue uniforms down by the river. Inspector Derwent raised his hand to his eyes and squinted.

"That looks like Clark down there. Hurst must have confirmed what Connie told you. Let's go and see if they have found anything, unless of course you are too tired, Miss Peto. It has been a busy afternoon."

"Not at all, Inspector," replied Dorothy quickly. She

wouldn't miss seeing what they might have found for the world.

A few moments later, they were down by the river. There were several barges moored close by; their occupants peering out the windows, watching proceedings. Sergeant Clark was standing next to a group of uniformed officers. Handcuffed to him was a young man, with his sleeves rolled up and wearing work trousers. They were all peering at something lying on the grass. As she got closer, Dorothy could see it was a gold fob watch. Sergeant Clark raised his hat when he saw them.

"Sir, Miss Peto. I finally got Hurst here to admit to being with his young lady on the night Hector was killed and the rest of their stories matched up," he said with a nod to the young man by his side. "One of our officers has been to speak with Mr Hurst's neighbour in Fulham. She recalled seeing the two of them arrive a little before midnight and leave at around half past four. The lady is a widow who spends much time at her window."

"Nosy old thing more like," muttered Jack then winced as Sergeant Clark elbowed him the ribs.

"Just as well for you, lad."

Dorothy studied Jack Hurst with interest. He was tall and heavily built with short dark hair, and he was eyeing the inspector suspiciously.

"Is this the watch you threw into the river?" the inspector asked him.

"It looks like it," replied Jack, earning himself another sharp jab to the ribs from Sergeant Clark. "It looks like it, sir."

The inspector nodded. "You found it quickly. Good work, Clark."

"We didn't exactly find it, sir. Someone beat us to it." He pointed towards the nearest barge and the old man sitting on the deck scowling at them. "Murdo Channing and his family have been moored here for the past four nights. They found the watch and a silver candlestick."

"I don't want no trouble," the man on the barge called out as he stepped on to the riverbank with one long stride.

"Neither do we," replied Inspector Derwent evenly. "How did that watch come to be in your possession?"

"Like I told your man over there, early Sunday morning just as we was getting up, we heard something hit the edge of the boat, then a splash and the sound of running feet. When I came outside there was no sign of them. I got my net out and started dredging. The watch came up straight away, so I thought I'd keep going, see if anything else was trapped down there between our boats. That's when we found a candlestick."

"And where is the candlestick now?"

"I sold it and the chain for the watch. Couldn't get rid of that though; the face is all smashed in."

"Who did you sell the candlestick and watch chain to?"

"Don't recall his name."

"Of course you don't," replied the inspector with an edge to his voice. "But you only heard one splash? Not another one earlier?"

"Just the one."

The inspector pointed back to Jack Hurst.

"Do you recall seeing that young man loitering around

here on Saturday evening?"

"Can't say I do."

"Did you see anyone behaving suspiciously?"

"I mind my own business. Others should do the same."

The inspector sighed. "Thank you for your time, Mr Channing."

"Seems a lot of trouble for a broken watch," the man muttered as he stepped back on to his boat.

"All right, Hurst, you are free to go."

"Free to go and fight for my country."

"Watch your lip, lad," chided Sergeant Clark as he removed the handcuffs. Jack made a big fuss of rubbing his wrists as he quickly strode away. Sergeant Clark quietly started murmuring that he still thought Hurst was shifty, while Inspector Derwent replied that they didn't have enough evidence to hold him. Dorothy was only half listening. She was watching Jack and the figure standing in the distance beneath a tree, waiting for him. Dorothy silently raised her hand. Connie did the same and mouthed the words 'thank you'.

As Dorothy looked away, a flash of crimson caught her eye. The barge farthest away had cast off and was moving downriver. Without really knowing why, Dorothy began moving down the towpath, straining her eyes to try to see who was on board, but the barge was chugging away too quickly. By standing on her tiptoes she managed to make out the name just before it disappeared under the bridge. It was called *Lady Elizabeth*.

Dorothy turned to the old man sitting on the boat nearest her.

"Who owns that boat, the *Lady Elizabeth*?" she asked.

"Can't say as I know," he replied not looking up from the net he was mending.

"Does it often moor here?" she persisted, but was met with another shrug of the shoulders.

"Maybe it does. Maybe it doesn't."

Resigned to the fact he wasn't going to give her any information, she left him and returned to where the inspector and sergeant were still discussing the smashed watch.

"Is there any chance you'll find the other candlestick?" she asked.

The inspector shook his head. "I'll set some of our men on to it, Miss Peto, but it's highly unlikely. These river people are a secretive lot. They abide by their own rules, often only speak their own Romany language. We are lucky they have told us this much." He raised his hat. "Thank you for your assistance today, Miss Peto. I wish you a pleasant evening."

Dorothy took that to mean she was being dismissed. Reluctantly, she began to walk away, occasionally glancing over her shoulder at the two detectives who were still deep in conversation.

It was still very warm and she could feel her shirt sticking to her back as she trudged back to Bloomsbury. Taking the omnibus would have been quicker but each one she saw was crammed with workers heading home; besides walking helped her think. As she passed the end of Cheyne Row, she considering going to see if Connie had returned, then thought better of it. It was quite possible only Gerald would be at the house, and she didn't want to find herself alone with him. She was certain he was involved in his uncle's death, but the inspector insisted on believing his alibi. That meant only Mrs Platt and Duckworth had been in the house when Hector was killed. She couldn't imagine Mrs Platt being a killer any more than she could Emily. Duckworth had been foolish to steal the candlestick and he clearly had many flaws, but surely murder wasn't one of them.

That would mean an intruder had killed Hector, someone who knew him well enough to use his routine of feeding the birds to try to disguise their crime. She thought Inspector Derwent had been teasing her when he mentioned Arnold Pearson could be a suspect, but was it possible he had acted to protect Emily? The two of them were clearly close. Perhaps Hector's death had nothing to do with the will. Perhaps Pearson killed Hector out of revenge for making Emily marry the dreadful Gerald.

Chapter Ten

WHEN SHE TURNED the key in her front door, she could hear music playing once again. Raymond must be home. She hurried into the sitting room. Her brother half-smiled when he saw her.

"Hello, old girl. I was hoping you'd come home before I have to catch my train."

He was leaning back in the chair, his eyes were half closed and a cigarette was clamped between his lips. On the table in front of him was an overflowing ashtray, a pile of gramophone records and a cricket bat.

"Raymond! When did you arrive home?" she asked hurrying over to hug him. He opened his eyes and reached up to hug her back.

"A few hours ago."

"How was Lady Sledmere?"

Raymond took a drag on his cigarette and exhaled slowly. "I'd always found her to be a rather cold, distant mother, but when I told her, she simply crumbled in front of me. It was quite appalling to see. As if all the life had left her too."

"The poor, poor woman," murmured Dorothy.

"I really didn't know what to say. I just sat there like a chump while she wept."

"I'm sure she appreciated you being there and telling her rather than receiving the telegram alone."

"At least I could intercept that and, as George's executor, I could set the wheels in motion with the family's solicitor, take the burden away from his mother."

"George made you his executor? I didn't know that."

"We each made wills during our last year at Cambridge. It seemed rather a joke at the time. I witnessed his signature and agreed to be his executor and vice versa. Naturally, he had rather more to leave than me. His twelve-year-old second cousin is now the new Lord Sledmere and inherits the whole estate."

"But he left you these?" she asked pointing to the records that she now recognised as some of George's favourites that he had brought back from their trip to New York.

Raymond shook his head. "No. He left all his personal effects to his mother. Besides, legally a witness isn't allowed to be a beneficiary. Lady Sledmere gave them to me. It was jolly kind of her." He picked up the cricket bat. "George scored a century with this when we beat Trinity, do you remember?"

Dorothy nodded. She and the rest of her family had cheered Raymond and George on at the university cricket match. Had it really only been three years ago? Raymond stood up and stubbed out his cigarette.

"I should change and shave before I leave for the station," he said.

"I'll make you a cup of tea," offered Dorothy as he walked out the room, but she couldn't be sure he was listening.

After saying goodbye and managing not to cry, Dorothy curled up on the sofa and thought about what Raymond had told her. Surely someone who had studied law, even briefly, would know the difference between a share certificate and someone's last will and testament, and that a witness to a will could not be someone who was due to inherit. If that was the case, then it wouldn't matter if Gerald had seen the details of the will or not, as he claimed. As soon as he witnessed Hector's signature, he would know he had been disinherited.

THE NEXT MORNING, Dorothy was sipping her second cup of tea, wishing Raymond could have stayed longer, when there was a cheerful rat-a-tat-tat on the front door. She knew who it was immediately.

"Morning, Dorothy dear," said Nina, giving her a hug as she bustled through the door and into the sitting room. "Where on earth did you get to yesterday afternoon? Once I'd calmed down, I went back to the office, but nobody knew where you were."

"I'm sorry. I followed you outside, but then I'm afraid I got caught up in the Hector Gaskill case," replied Dorothy, feeling herself blush. In truth, with all the excitement surrounding Connie and Duckworth, she had forgotten all about Nina and Margaret's disagreement.

"Good. I was worried you might be wallowing about George. I know how fond you were of him. Has Derwent arrested the dastardly Gerald yet?"

"No, unfortunately not. He seems determined to believe

his alibi."

"Ah well, I'm sure you'll help him see the light. Now to business. Margaret has arranged a vote at Caxton Hall this afternoon."

"So soon?" she asked in surprise.

"Mary has been egging her on. I imagine she loves the idea of DORA. Yet more rules and regulations for her to enforce. Therefore, we need to rally the troops."

"Are you sure, Nina?"

"What do you mean?"

"Are you sure you want to press the matter so forcefully? What will you do if you lose the vote?"

Nina stared at her blankly for a moment and Dorothy realised the thought of such a thing had never occurred to her.

"How can you think I would lose? You've read the newspapers. The Defence of the Realm Act is a direct attack on women."

"The government is trying to do something to stop the spread of venereal disease. You know as well as I do that cases of syphilis have shot up."

"Then target the men who visit the prostitutes. Why are women always seen as the guilty party? It's like being back in Marlborough Street Police Court before the war. How many times when a woman had been abused did the lawyers or even the judge argue that it was somehow her fault? 'She provoked him.' 'He couldn't help himself.' You catalogued those cases alongside me. I can't believe you don't agree with me, Dorothy!"

"I do agree with you. These new laws are unfair, but

many of our members, including those from the Women's Freedom League decided to put our own beliefs to one side while the country is at war. You, Mary, Margaret and I sat opposite Sir Edward Henry and promised to uphold and enforce all the laws in the land, not just those we agreed with," Dorothy reminded her gently.

Nina bristled. "And I kept my promise but these new laws are a step too far. I simply cannot bring myself to enforce them. They are against everything I stand for."

Dorothy nodded her head but remained silent. She knew it was useless to try to change her friend's mind, but she certainly didn't share her confidence that she would win the vote.

Despite her misgivings, she did as Nina had asked and spent the morning 'rallying the troops'. She visited the WPV patrols at King's Cross, St Pancras and Euston Stations then went to Regent's Park. After a restorative cup of tea in a café on Regent Street, she headed towards St James's Park. She should have time to speak to the women patrolling there and in Green Park and Hyde Park before the meeting.

As she crossed Trafalgar Square, she decided on impulse to make a quick detour to Ciro's. It was still early. If Bessie was there, she might not have started drinking yet. Perhaps she would speak more openly to her without the inspector present. Even if she didn't change her story, she might open up a little and tell her what she and Gerald had talked about. He may have let slip to her that he knew he'd been written out of the will—that might at least give him a motive. However, as soon as she rounded the corner on to Orange Street, she almost bumped into Eric Curtis. He was dressed in a dark navy suit and hat and had a newspaper tucked under his arm. In the daylight, his complexion looked almost grey and there were dark circles under his yes. It seemed, like Gerald, he was more of a creature of the night.

"Ah, Miss Peto, what a pleasant surprise. I knew you wouldn't be able to stay away. Here to enjoy a pre-lunch martini no doubt. Don't worry, I shan't report you for drinking on duty."

Also, like Gerald, his smile was more of a leer. Dorothy didn't like the way he'd managed to find out her name either. Inspector Derwent had been careful not to introduce her to him.

"Good afternoon, Mr Curtis," she replied. "Actually, I was hoping to discover a little more of what happened here on Saturday night."

"Ah I see you are enjoying playing at being a detective. Well, I've always been rather fond of role-play myself. Ask away."

Dorothy could feel her face beginning to burn. This really wasn't the encounter she had hoped for but talking to one of the people providing Gerald with his alibi was an opportunity too good to miss.

"When Gerald dined with his uncle on Saturday evening, he also witnessed his uncle's signature on a legal document."

"I don't recall him mentioning any document—legal or otherwise—unless you count the times he has wished he'd never signed his marriage certificate to Saint Emily. Usually after a few whiskies have been enjoyed."

"Saint Emily?"

"The poor girl must be a saint. Living under the same

roof all those years as the man who bankrupted her father and caused him to throw himself off the top of the stock exchange. Hector only took her in because his name would have been blackened in the city even further if Silas Judd's orphaned daughter had ended up in the workhouse."

Dorothy frowned. Mr Pearson had omitted to mention these details when he'd spoken to her, but she didn't want to let herself be distracted.

"This particular legal document was, in fact, his uncle's last will and testament. I understand Mr Gaskill trained as a lawyer briefly. Surely he would be able to recognise even part of a will and understand that if he was a witness, he would not be a benefactor."

Curtis gave a nonchalant shake of his head. "I'm not at all sure he would. I don't recall him attending many lectures. They took place a little early in the day for him."

"A jury might not believe that."

Curtis narrowed his eyes, but a smile still played on his lips. "Very good, Miss Peto. When you aren't pretending to be in the police, do you pretend to be a lawyer or even a judge perhaps?"

Dorothy could feel herself blushing again. He seemed to enjoy her discomfort.

"It is quite possible Gerald realised he had been disinherited without seeing this new will; however, I would argue that would give him cause to ensure his uncle lived, not be a reason to kill him. A living wealthy relative can always be persuaded to change their will again. A dead one cannot."

He was using the same reasoning the inspector had, but Dorothy pushed on. "Is that what you advised him, Mr

Curtis? Perhaps you also gave him advice about where to say he'd been when the police came looking for him?"

It was as close as she dare get to asking him if he had lied, but he saw through her clumsy attempt. He treated her to another of his snake-like grins.

"Gerald never asked for my advice. If he had, I would have told him what I used to tell all my clients: 'Honesty is the best policy'. I can see from your charmingly readable face that you don't believe me, and you are quite right not to. I'm sure I've lied many times over the years. Assured anxious wives their husbands were drinking with me rather than entertaining another young lady. Promised creditors their cheque was in the post when in fact it was resting on my desk. Told my doctor I only drink occasionally. However, I would draw the line at providing a false alibi to a Scotland Yard detective inspector, and risk being asked to perjure myself, even for Gerry. Now, perhaps you will excuse me."

He turned to go.

"I was hoping to speak to Miss Shelton too. Do you happen to know if she is in your establishment?"

He paused and glanced at his watch. "It's a little early for a drink, even for Bessie. You are of course very welcome to come in and wait. She's bound to make an appearance at some point. We could share a bottle of champagne and you could interrogate me a little more."

"No thank you. Do you have her home address?"

He laughed, as if she had made a clever joke. Dorothy didn't think she'd ever met a man she liked less. It really was little wonder he and Gerald were friends.

"I'm afraid I don't. Bessie is one of life's drifters, shall we say. She doesn't like to stay in the same place too long. It must be in the blood."

"I see. Well thank you for your time, Mr Curtis."

"Not at all. The pleasure was all mine, Miss Peto."

He strolled into the club, whistling to himself and leaving Dorothy on the pavement feeling foolish and relieved that neither Inspector Derwent nor any of the other detectives had witnessed her clumsy attempt to gain information about Gerald Gaskill. The inspector saying he had waited for her until he questioned Emily had gone to her head. She might be able to get the likes of Connie and Emily to confide in her, but it was clear she had a lot to learn when it came to interviewing men like Eric Curtis.

DOROTHY SHIFTED UNCOMFORTABLY in her seat. It was a little after four o'clock that afternoon and she was on the front row of Caxton Hall. It was the first time she had been here since the ill-fated meeting of the Women's Freedom League when Nina had been arrested. It was also the day when they had first met Mary. Both events seemed like a very long time ago now. Working together with Margaret and Mary, they had achieved many things she and Nina had only dared dream of, yet today that could all come to an end. Whoever lost the vote, whether it be Margaret or Nina, they were bound to resign. Without either woman, the WPV wouldn't be the same.

Sitting behind and alongside her were around fifty members of the London WPV and a few more from other parts of the country, who were in the capital for training. Dorothy knew them all; indeed she had enrolled many of them. As they filed in, she had turned to smile and greet them, but very few had managed to look her in the eye. Everyone knew how close she and Nina were. Perhaps that was why nobody had really wanted to discuss today's meeting with her either. Almost all her enquiries had been met with vague responses. One or two women, who were more forthcoming, had said they agreed with Nina 'in principle', but also added 'but it's like Mary says, Margaret is the appointed commandant and does provide all the funding'.

This had worried Dorothy. She wondered if Mary had spoken to them and implied that the funding for WPV might disappear if today's vote didn't go Margaret's way. She certainly wouldn't put it past her and that thought added to her feelings of discomfort. Mary had also let it be known that she was warming to the idea of members of the WPV being seconded into the regular police and receiving a wage. Dorothy wasn't convinced by this apparent change of heart, but it might win over a few undecided voters today. Mary was very proud of Margaret being the commandant. If the vote went Nina's way, Margaret would step down and so Mary would do whatever she could to ensure that didn't happen.

Up on the stage Nina stood at the lectern while Margaret and Mary sat behind her. Nina had been speaking against enforcing the new laws for almost twenty minutes now. She sounded as passionate as ever, but Margaret and Mary remained stony-faced. Dorothy agreed with every word Nina was saying, but she sensed that the rest of the room, which contained many non-WFL members, were not being persuaded. Even those who were members of the league and who, at one time, would have given Nina their unwavering support whenever she spoke, today just sat in polite silence.

"The sight of women whom these hypocrites call unfortunate, tried by a court martial in England, their rights snatched away from them, is utterly sickening," Nina continued. "We should take no part in it."

"No order, however distasteful, can be shirked. We are at war," interjected Mary loudly. She had clearly had enough of listening quietly. Looking a little shocked at being interrupted, Nina paused and was about to argue back, but at that moment Margaret rose to her feet and stepped forward.

"Thank you for speaking so eloquently, Miss Boyle," she said firmly and reluctantly Nina returned to her seat. "Ladies," continued Margaret, "you know I believe we should co-operate with the men; indeed it is what the three of us here on the stage before you promised Sir Edward Henry when he first agreed to allow us to form this organisation. We gave him our word that we would work to uphold all the laws of this land, not just those that suited us. However, the decision rests with you. May I therefore please ask those of you against enforcing any curfew, as outlined in the Defence of the Realm Act, to raise your hand."

The hall was silent as only Nina and Dorothy raised their hands. Dorothy watched helplessly as Nina's shoulders slumped and a small, satisfied smile crossed Mary's lips.

"And those of you in favour of enforcing such a curfew," Margaret continued.

The rest of the women in the hall raised their hands.

"Thank you, ladies. That seems to settle the matter. The Women Police Volunteers will work to enforce any curfew as part of the Defence of the Realm Act," said Margaret and turned to Nina, who was already on her feet.

"Commandant Damer Dawson," she began, "I wish to tender my resignation, not only as the deputy commandant of the Women Police Volunteers, but as a member of this organisation, with immediate effect."

There were a few gasps of surprise and sharp intakes of breath. Horrified, Dorothy leapt to her feet.

"Oh, Nina, please don't! This is a democratic organisation. Surely, we can disagree and still work together."

Margaret ignored Dorothy's intervention and instead replied to Nina. "On behalf of the Women Police Volunteers, I accept your resignation, Miss Boyle, and thank you for your service."

Nina bowed her head slightly. She knew when she'd been beaten. Dorothy bit her lip. Deep down she had always feared this moment might come, ever since that first meeting with Sir Edward, when Mary manoeuvred Margaret into the position of commander. Nina must be terribly hurt, especially as so many previous WFL members had failed to support her, but with a brave smile she addressed the audience.

"I am sorry I won't be with you for the rest of your journey. Goodbye, ladies, and good luck."

Then she marched down the steps and out through the hall with her head held high, but Dorothy could see the tears glistening in her eyes. Margaret silently watched her go and as the door swung closed with a thud, she addressed the audience once more.

"If there are no objections, I should like to propose Miss Mary Sophie Allen as my new deputy?"

The room broke into applause and Mary, smiling broadly stood up, nodded and waved her thanks, then shook Margaret by the hand. Dorothy felt her heart sink and exchanged a worried glance with Jean Bagster, her old friend from the Women's Freedom League. Even though she had voted against Nina, Jean was looking less than happy with the sudden turn of events. However, Margaret hadn't finished yet.

"Following these changes in personnel and based on the fact that many of our members may soon begin earning a wage for their sterling work, I propose we also change the name of our organisation and from now on be known as the Women's Police Service."

"Hear! Hear!" seconded Mary, loudly, amid more clapping. Dorothy had heard enough. It was as if they were trying to erase everything Nina had achieved and claim it as their own. She stood up and dashed out into the street, desperate to find her friend, but there was no sign of her. She spent the rest of the afternoon and evening looking everywhere she could think of: the Eustace Miles Restaurant, Alan's Tea Rooms, The Gardenia restaurant, even the reading room in the British Library, but there was no sign of Nina anywhere.

Chapter Eleven

I T WAS ALMOST eight o'clock that evening when Dorothy finally tracked Nina down to her flat in Bayswater. Her friend was such a social creature, she hadn't thought to look there at first. Now she was worried that Nina was so upset, she was hiding herself away. It took three rings on the doorbell before Nina answered the door with a cigarette in one hand and a bundle of clothes in the other.

"Hello there, Dorothy. Come in, but you must excuse the mess. I'm in the middle of packing."

To Dorothy's relief, she looked and sounded remarkably cheerful. She stepped through the door and then over two piles of books. She'd never known the flat to be anything other than a mess. Organised chaos, Nina liked to call it.

"Are you going away somewhere?" she asked as she followed Nina through into her bedroom where a large trunk lay open on the floor.

"Yes. Serbia," replied Nina.

"Serbia! What on earth for?"

"I'm going to be a nurse. The poor old Balkans have been rather forgotten since war broke out. Everyone has been concentrating on the Western front, but fighting is still going out there and they need nurses."

Dorothy stared at her in disbelief. If she wasn't actually watching her friend throw her belongings into a trunk, she would have assumed she was joking.

"Don't you think you are being a little rash, Nina? I know you must be terribly upset about the meeting, but Serbia?"

"Losing the vote was a blow I admit, but even if it had gone my way, I couldn't have worked with Margaret and Mary much longer, perhaps it was a blessing in disguise. After speaking with you this morning, I considered what I should do if I should lose the vote and then I remembered Mabel Grouitch. Do you recall we heard her speak last year?"

Dorothy nodded. She had been very impressed with the charming and energetic wife of the Serbian Foreign Secretary, who had set up the Serbian Relief Fund. At the beginning of the war, everyone's focus had been on what was happening in France and Belgium, and their Balkan ally was in danger of being completely forgotten, but thanks to Mabel's efforts that hadn't happened.

"Well, I was at one of her fundraising events last month and the two of us chatted afterwards. I told her how I felt quite drawn to her brave country, fighting alone and sandwiched between its enemies Bulgaria and the evil old Austro-Hungarian Empire. Then Mabel explained that in spring this year, the Russians, British, French, Italians and Greeks had all sent reinforcements for a planned offensive, but it had not been a success. There were over twenty-five thousand British casualties alone and such an increase in casualties inevitably led to an increase in the need for nurses. So, I started thinking and with my background of nursing in South Africa, I thought I should answer the call. I went to see Mabel as soon as I left Caxton Hall."

As Dorothy listened, she could hear the excitement in Nina's voice and her eyes were gleaming brightly. Serbia was clearly going to be her next obsession. There was next to no chance she would change her mind, but Dorothy had to at least try.

"But how will you get there? Won't it be dangerous? How will you manage? You don't speak Serbian or know anything of their culture or religion."

"No, but I expect I'll get by. It will be good to feel useful again, like I'm making a difference," she declared as she flung anther handful of clothes into the trunk. She turned and grinned at Dorothy. "Why not come with me? We could have such an adventure."

Dorothy shook her head with a sinking heart. "No, I couldn't go, Nina. I'm not a nurse and I'm not as brave as you."

"Nonsense," her friend said with a laugh.

"Are you sure you won't change your mind?"

Nina paused for a moment and her smile faded just a little. "No. I couldn't bear staying here, seeing all of you on patrol and not being part of it. I sail tomorrow."

Dorothy reached over and hugged her friend. She understood Nina's decision, but she was going to miss her terribly.

IF IT WAS possible, Southampton felt even more chaotic than London. So many troops on the dockside waiting to board the ships that would take them across the Channel and so many friends and family there to wave their brave boys off. In amongst them all, being pushed and shoved from side to side, were Dorothy and Nina in her new nurse's uniform courtesy of the Serbian embassy. She had made Dorothy promise to come and wave her off. Not that Dorothy needed much persuading.

The two of them had left Waterloo at dawn. The rocking of the train threatened to send Dorothy to sleep and she had to fight to stay awake. She'd been awake all night thinking about how much she would miss her friend. Her encounter with Eric was still unsettling her too. Normally she would have told Nina all about it but her friend was so excited she didn't want to spoil their last few hours together talking about Gerald and Eric. Despite her best efforts, she had begun to feel herself nodding off, until she was suddenly nudged awake by Nina, who was reading the first edition of that morning's newspaper.

"Look, Dorothy!" she almost squealed in delight. "Edith has done it!"

"Who?" asked Dorothy, opening her eyes and squinting at the article Nina had thrust in front of her.

"Edith Smith, the woman from Grantham I told you about. Look, she's done it. She's been attested."

Dorothy sat up and read the few lines of text tucked away in the corner of page eight. "Yesterday in Grantham…Chief Constable Casburn… Oh my goodness. It's true! She's been given the power to arrest and a warrant card and been granted a constable's wage." She continued reading. "In light of Mrs Smith's sterling work and the very real difference she is making to Grantham, many of the town's dignitaries wrote to say they would like to see her take on a more official role…since Mrs Smith had started these strange patrols of hers, there had been a remarkable drop in the complaints regarding lewd behaviour in the town's public spaces. When asked about the guidelines from the Home Office regarding the Women Police Volunteers and how they should not be given the power to arrest, Chief Constable Casburn referred to the letters he had received. 'I don't think there can be any doubt that we understand the needs of our town more than some anonymous civil servants in Whitehall'." Dorothy chuckled. "More like he knows he is far more likely to bump into one of these local dignitaries and have to explain himself to them rather than a member of the Home Office."

"I quite agree, Dorothy, but isn't it wonderful! I knew those letters would do the trick. I take this to be a very good omen for my trip and I can leave the WPV with my head held high. We have achieved something marvellous."

Dorothy had been able to think of little else for the rest of the journey. Thoughts about Hector Gaskill and even the imminent departure of Nina were taken over by the idea that Edith could be just the first of them to become a proper policewoman. A precedent had been set. There was nothing to stop the same thing happening to her.

NOW, AS THEY edged through the crowds, her eyes wandered towards the ship that had only recently docked and the soldiers who were disembarking. They were some of the wounded returning from the Battle of Loos. They all looked so utterly tattered and tired. Some were on crutches, others were heavily bandaged, then came the stretchers carrying those even more seriously injured. Dorothy couldn't help thinking about George. Perhaps these brave men had served alongside him.

Suddenly, a loud voice behind them said, "Well, well, little sister, I wasn't expecting a welcoming committee."

Both women spun round. Standing there was Captain Patrick Boyle, Nina's older brother. He was short, stocky and spoke with a slight accent from his time in South Africa. Fighting there during the Boer War had also left him needing to wear an eyepatch. Despite his alarming appearance and slightly brusque manner, Dorothy liked him very much. She watched as Nina threw her arms around him.

"Patrick, how wonderful to see you. What are you doing here? Are you injured?"

He lifted his bandaged left hand.

"Barely a scratch, but my regiment suffered heavy casualties. Those of us who survived have been granted a week's leave before we regroup."

"Were you at the Battle of Loos?" asked Dorothy.

He nodded.

"We read about it in the newspaper. How was it really?" asked Nina.

"Utterly bloody. Excuse my language, Miss Peto."

"Not at all. I'm pleased you aren't badly injured, Captain."

"Thank you. So, what brings the two of you here?"

"I'm off to Serbia. To be a nurse there," explained Nina.

Her brother raised an eyebrow, in a way that reminded Dorothy of Inspector Derwent. "Nursing in the Balkans? Who do you think you are, little sister? Florence Nightingale? The last I heard, you were planning on becoming a superintendent at Scotland Yard."

"Plans change, Patrick," Nina replied airily.

Dorothy smiled to herself. Nina and Patrick teased each other mercilessly, but she knew how close they were. They had lost their brother Michael in South Africa. He had died from his injuries because there weren't enough doctors and nurses at the field hospital to treat his wounds. When Nina heard the news, she had given up her job as a journalist in Cape Town and immediately volunteered to be a nurse. She might not have been able to save Michael, but she had been determined to do all she could to help other wounded soldiers.

By now Nina was at the front of the queue. Dorothy and Patrick both hugged her goodbye then stood and watched her walk up the wobbly gangplank. Then they waited for her to appear on the deck, her new nurse's cape flapping in the breeze.

The two of them stood side by side waving goodbye as the boat slowly edged out of the harbour. Dorothy brushed away a tear with the back of her hand. She was going to miss Nina terribly. Patrick silently handed her his handkerchief. He was about to turn and go when Dorothy thought of something.

"I don't suppose you knew Lieutenant Paul Gaskill, Captain Boyle?"

He looked at her in surprise. "Yes, I did. He was in my company. A fine soldier and a good man. A terrible waste. I've written to his grandfather and his wife. I wanted them to know he was killed instantaneously, that he didn't suffer at all. I hoped it may help ease their grief."

"That was kind of you. Unfortunately, his grandfather died a few days ago too."

"What a strange coincidence, but perhaps a blessing that he didn't live to hear the news."

"I'm sorry, Captain, did you say, his wife?" she asked wondering if she had misheard him.

"Yes. Jessica. Nice girl. They were married just before we left Belton Park—our training camp. It was rather a rushed affair. I was one of their witnesses."

"Where is Jessica now?" she asked. This was the first she'd heard of Paul having a wife.

"Still up north as far as I know. I'm sorry, Miss Peto, but I really must go. It was awfully nice seeing you again. And don't worry about Nina. She is more than capable of taking care of herself. Good day."

Dorothy watched him stride away, her mind beginning to race. Did Hector know his grandson was married? Is that why he wanted to change his will? Did anyone else know about the marriage? None of the servants had mentioned it. Neither had Gerald or Emily. What could the existence of a wife, another possible beneficiary, mean for the investigation? She turned back to give Nina one last wave goodbye, but the ship had already sailed out of sight.

IT WAS GROWING late when Dorothy returned to London, but the first thing she did was go straight to Scotland Yard. Despite the hour, she found Inspector Derwent in his office, sitting at his desk with his door open.

"Paul Gaskill was married," she blurted out.

He looked up. "Good evening, Miss Peto. Do come in and sit down."

"Paul was married," she repeated flopping down on to the chair opposite him. She was quite out of breath after hurrying from the station.

"How do you know?" he asked calmly.

"I bumped into one of his superior officers when I was waving Nina off in Southampton."

"Of course you did. Where and when did this marriage take place?" he asked picking up a pencil.

"Just before he left for the front, while he was still at his training camp."

"I was really hoping for an exact date and the name of a church."

"Oh I'm sorry, I should have asked Captain Boyle but I was rather taken by surprise when he told me. I was wondering about it all the way here. What if the letter Hector Gaskill received was from his grandson telling him about his marriage? That could have been what prompted him to change his will, and I was wondering if it might affect the inheritance somehow."

"You may well be correct. I'll ask Sergeant Clark to look into it."

"Oh," said Dorothy in disappointment, "I thought it was rather exciting news. Don't you think Paul's marriage could be seen as a motive, the catalyst for someone to act?"

"At the moment, I think it is more of a complication than a catalyst. We don't know for sure it took place." He held up his hand as she opened her mouth to protest. "Or that anyone here in London knew."

"I suppose that is true," she said reluctantly. "My ideas were just speculation. Has there been any progress in the investigation?"

"If you mean have we found Hector Gaskill's killer yet, the answer is no. Mr Duckworth was granted bail by the magistrate this morning and he is now residing with his sister at the pub she runs in Hackney."

"I don't think it's a good idea for him to live in a pub, with his problems with alcohol," she replied with a frown.

"And I don't think it's a good idea for him to have been released at all but there was little point in us pressing charges after Gerald informed us he was unwilling to make a statement or give evidence."

"Why did Gerald say that? Surely, Duckworth must be the prime suspect for his uncle's murder."

The inspector looked a little embarrassed as he shuffled the papers in front of him.

"He was, until Willerby kindly reminded me that Hector Gaskill was struck by someone who is right-handed and Duckworth is left-handed, so there we have it. He may be a thief, but not a killer. At least not in this case."

"Oh, that is disappointing," agreed Dorothy, thinking he sounded more tired than irritated. "Nothing else?"

"Following our visit to Chelsea Embankment, I believe Jack Hurst has now joined his regiment. Connie and Mrs

Platt are currently still at Cheyne Row, as is Gerald Gaskill, and Emily is still conspicuous in her absence. Mr Pearson informs me that he has applied for probate regarding Hector's estate. There, I think you are fully up to date with proceedings, Miss Peto."

"Thank you, Inspector," replied Dorothy meekly. "I know I've only been away a day, but well…I suppose after helping Margaret find the body, I do feel rather involved in the case."

"That has been noted, Miss Peto," replied the inspector.

"In fact, I tried to speak to Bessie again yesterday morning, but she wasn't at Ciro's. Instead, I bumped into that awful Eric Curtis."

The inspector stared at her for a moment. "You went to Ciro's alone?" There was a coldness in his voice that she hadn't heard before.

"Yes, although I didn't enter the place. I spoke to Mr Curtis in the street outside," she replied beginning to feel nervous.

"And what passed between the two of you?"

"I was trying to find out if Gerald knew he was witnessing a will. I thought it strange that a man with some legal training wouldn't realise and, if he did, he would know a witness could not be a beneficiary…" She trailed off as the inspector's expression got sterner and sterner.

"Did it not occur to you, Miss Peto, that not only was a man as cunning and astute as Curtis unlikely to divulge such information, but that he was also likely to warn his friend that he is still very much a suspect of ours? We had hoped that Duckworth's arrest would allow him to relax. When criminals relax, they make mistakes."

"I'm sorry," she stammered. "You see I caught a glimpse of crimson on one of the barges, which made me think about Bessie, and I thought you had ruled out Gerald, but I was sure he was involved."

"I had not ruled him out. I had merely been prioritising the suspects we have in order of the evidence against them. Sergeant Brook has been following Gerald Gaskill these last twenty-four hours but he may well have been wasting his time, if Gaskill is now on his guard, thanks to your encounter with Curtis."

"I'm sorry," she repeated, tears beginning to prick her eyes.

He wasn't shouting but his icy tone was far worse. He rose to his feet. "I think it's about time I headed home, Miss Peto. May I suggest you do the same."

Feeling wretched, Dorothy followed the inspector out through the warren of corridors in silence. When they stepped into the street, he finally spoke to her again. She was sure he was going to tell her to stay away from everyone involved in the case and not to darken his door again. Instead, he asked about Nina.

"Am I to understand Miss Boyle has gone abroad?" His tone was neutral once more.

"Yes, she has decided to go to Serbia. To nurse the wounded," replied Dorothy, taken aback. The inspector rarely enquired about her private life or her friends, but she was relieved for the change in subject.

"Nursing? I rather thought Miss Boyle was intent upon her mission to have women be accepted into the force and be given the power to arrest. Her campaign seemed to be succeeding. I understand one of your volunteers has been attested up north somewhere. In Lancashire, was it? No, Lincolnshire."

Dorothy looked at him in surprise. "You heard about that? Yes, Nina saw it as rather a triumph. A last hurrah she called it, but it wasn't enough to keep her here. She disagreed with Mary and Margaret about the WPV being used to enforce some aspects of the Defence of the Realm Act."

"Yes, I imagine Miss Boyle would find it difficult to support some of the new laws. Actually, I would have imagined you would have felt the same, Miss Peto."

"I do but not enough to leave the WPV. I did promise Sir Edward Henry I would uphold all the laws of the land, or perhaps I'm just not as brave as Nina. Either way, I shall miss her terribly."

The inspector nodded but made no further comment. Instead, he raised his cane to summon a taxicab to take her home. He opened the door for her and she gratefully sank into the back seat of the cab. After giving the driver her address, she turned to wave the inspector goodbye, but he had already disappeared.

Chapter Twelve

THE NEXT MORNING, although still upset and unsettled by the inspector's reprimand, Dorothy decided to pay Mr Pearson a visit. She was sure he would be more interested in her news about Paul's possible marriage and despite Inspector Derwent's lack of enthusiasm, she was confident it must be important to the investigation. She found the lawyer at his desk, frowning at a stack of legal documents in front of him and steadily working his way through a large box of Cadbury's Milk Tray chocolates. He stood and smiled broadly when his doddery clerk showed her in.

"Miss Peto, how delightful to see you again. Please sit down. How may I help you?"

"Mr Pearson, may I ask you a hypothetical question?"

The solicitor chuckled and Dorothy noticed chocolate had melted on to his shirt cuffs and there were several smudges on the document he was working on.

"Of course, young lady. I spend most of my life dealing with the hypothetical."

"If Hector Gaskill had discovered his grandson was married, how do you think he would have reacted?" she asked politely waving away his offer of a chocolate.

The solicitor's eyes opened very wide. "Good Lord! Was

Paul married? So, that's why Hector wanted to change his will. I've been racking my brains trying to find a cause for his urgency."

"I think he found out about the marriage in the letter he received that morning from Paul but what I don't understand is why he would have burnt the letter."

Mr Pearson shrugged. "Acting in anger. Hector Gaskill was a traditionalist. He would have been furious to think Paul had married without permission and I'm assuming if the marriage was not announced formally that the young lady in question doesn't come from the sort of family Hector would have chosen for his grandson. Hector had a short fuse, as I mentioned before. He did not suffer fools gladly. But his anger was of the cold sort. However, Hector was also a pragmatic man. Knowing that his grandson could well be killed in action and that a child may already have been conceived, he would want to ensure that child, his great-grandchild, was provided for should the worst happen. So, he decided to write a new will, making his direct heirs a priority and cutting out anyone else whom may have hoped to benefit."

"I don't know about pragmatic. That sounds rather clinical, Mr Pearson," replied Dorothy. "To think of amending your will rather than, say, sending for your grandson's new wife, so you could meet her, reassure her. A new bride separated from her husband almost immediately when he is sent to the front would be in need of comfort."

Mr Pearson nodded thoughtfully.

"It's true but Hector was not an emotional man, Miss Peto. He had a tendency to see people as problems that needed solving rather than fellow beings with thoughts and feelings to be considered. Take poor Emily and her unfortunate situation. Hector wanted to settle Gerald down, so to speak and he didn't believe anyone else could be induced to marry Emily. He actually used the phrase 'two birds with one stone, Pearson' when I queried his decision." The lawyer shook his head at the memory. "He simply couldn't imagine anyone would see how special Emily was."

This last sentence he almost spoke to himself, and he seemed lost in his thoughts for a moment.

Dorothy gave a small cough. "Mr Pearson, in terms of inheritance, what does Paul having a wife mean? Does she have any claim on Hector's estate?"

The solicitor removed his glasses and rubbed his hand over his eyes. "Miss Peto, I can't tell you how many times I have admonished myself for allowing Hector to burn the old will and not make a copy of the new one. I allowed him to bully me and acted against my better judgement. Not for the first time I may add. But now, let me consider your particular question. It's actually rather a tricky problem. In this case the law is like comedy—it's all to do with timing." Dorothy smiled politely at his little joke and let him continue. "It would seem that Paul was killed before Hector, in which case the rules of intestate apply and Gerald, as the closest living relative inherits."

"Not Paul's wife?"

"No, only blood relatives, I'm afraid, Miss Peto. Of course, if Paul had died after his grandfather, the estate would have passed to him and upon his death to his heirs. Although I don't have his will, I assume he would have made one before leaving for the front. That needs to be looked into," he said making a note for himself in the open diary on his desk. Dorothy recalled Inspector Derwent had said something similar about soldiers being ordered to get their affairs in order. Sadly, it didn't help his widow and it looked like Gerald was still due to inherit the old man's fortune.

She left Mr Pearson's office and reluctantly headed towards Little George Street. She couldn't put off returning to the WPV offices, or WPS offices as she would have to start calling them, any longer. When she arrived, she wasn't surprised to find Mary had lost no time in changing the brass name plaque outside. She trudged up the steps. The place didn't feel the same now that Nina had gone. To make matters worse, she found that Mary had already taken over her old friend's desk opposite Margaret. The two of them looked up when they saw her.

Margaret gave a nervous cough. "Oh hello there, Dorothy. We wondered where you were. Nobody had seen you since the meeting?"

"You should have been on duty at Euston Station yesterday," added Mary.

Dorothy ignored her and addressed Margaret instead. "I was in Southampton seeing Nina off," replied Dorothy. "She decided to become a nurse in the Balkans seeing as she is no longer valued here."

"Honestly, who does she think she is? Florence Nightingale?" sniped Mary. She was echoing Patrick's words but without any of the underlying affection. "You could still have told us, Dorothy."

"May I remind you I am a volunteer, Mary, not a paid

employee," she snapped. "I haven't taken a day off in months and after everything Nina has done for me and the rest of us, I wanted to say goodbye properly. I felt I owed her that. However, perhaps you wish I had resigned too."

"Now, now, Dorothy dear," interrupted Margaret quickly. "That's not what we want at all. We are sorry about how things turned out with Nina and we both wish her well in her new venture, but speaking of travelling, how do you feel about a short trip up to Grantham?"

"Grantham? In Lincolnshire? Why?" asked Dorothy in surprise.

"Edith Smith, a member of the WPS there, has just been attested," explained Mary, stressing the new name of the organisation.

"Yes, I read about it."

Mary snorted loudly. "Don't try to tell us you didn't know about it already. The scheme has Nina's fingerprints all over it. I've always said she was a loose cannon. Not thinking of anyone her actions might upset."

"Who has she upset?" asked Dorothy.

"The usual suspects. McKenna isn't happy," Margaret began to explain, but Mary interrupted her.

"Poor Margaret was summoned to a meeting with Sir Edward Henry and Leonard Dunning, the chief of constabulary."

"It was rather an awkward meeting," admitted Margaret. "Dunning looked straight at me and told me he believed Casburn, the chief constable in Grantham, 'has apparently fallen into the hands of some strong women', although he also added that Edith Smith was 'perhaps a better man than he is' and Sir Henry did agree, a little reluctantly, that a precedent had been set."

Dorothy wished Nina could have heard this. She would have thrown her head back and howled with laughter, then declared they should go out and celebrate this triumph. Instead, Dorothy had Mary glowering across the desk at her.

"That's not the point," she snapped. "Nina's stunt could have destroyed much of our good work and the trust we have tried to build up with Scotland Yard and the Home Office," she continued. It was clear she was spoiling for an argument and for once Dorothy was happy to oblige, but Margaret must have seen the look on her face and quickly stepped in.

"Now, Dorothy dear. We also received a letter from Edith Smith herself. It seems she has some misgivings about the Defence of the Realm Act too."

She removed a letter from her drawer and handed it over.

"This is addressed to Nina," said Dorothy looking at the letter.

"Actually, it is addressed to the deputy commandant. I hold that position now, but as you were so close to Nina, we thought it might be best if you visit Mrs Smith and explain our position. Offer her some reassurance. After all, as the first of our number to be attested, it wouldn't do for her to go and resign."

Despite Margaret's protestation, was it possible they wanted to get her out of the way because she had supported Nina? Dorothy wasn't sure. It was a little over a year ago that the four of them had worked so closely together. Now everything seemed to have been thrown upside down.

"If that's what you want, Margaret, then of course I shall

go," she replied with a tight smile. Perhaps putting some distance between herself and Mary might be for the best. It would give her time to think.

THE NEXT DAY, Dorothy took the train up to Grantham. It was a long journey but she didn't mind. It was good to be away from the heat and dirt of London as well as Mary and Margaret for a while. Although it did mean missing out on any progress into the investigation of Hector Gaskill's murder. Perhaps after her disastrous attempt to interview Eric, that was a good thing too. She was certain that's what Inspector Derwent would be thinking.

She had a short wait in Birmingham for her connection on to Lincolnshire and while she was there, she bought a copy of the local newspaper from the boy on the platform. As she flicked through the pages, she discovered they too had reported the story of Edith being given the power to arrest. It was even accompanied by a photograph. The image was a little blurry, but it should help her identify the woman she was going to meet.

When she finally arrived in Grantham, it was late afternoon. The sun was shining brightly, but she was pleased to find it much cooler than in the capital. She stepped off the train in a cloud of steam. All around her swarmed young men in uniform wating to start their long journey to the front line. How cruel, thought Dorothy. To have to depart on such a perfect day. As she made her way along the platform, she realised she was attracting quite a lot of attention. There was much staring and nudging between the locals. People in the small Lincolnshire town were evidently not used to seeing women in uniform. Perhaps the photograph in the newspaper wouldn't be necessary after all.

After checking in at the Angel and Royal Hotel and spending a few moments unpacking and washing her hands and face, she set off in search of Edith Smith. Before leaving London, she had written Mrs Smith's address down from the letter sent to Nina. Dorothy asked the elderly man at the reception desk for directions and set off, but she had only been walking for a few moments when she spotted the lady she was looking for. Edith was dressed in the same blue uniform as herself. A short, slightly plump, bespectacled woman with curly grey hair, she was marching purposefully through the gates of the local park. Dorothy followed her, then stopped by a bench to watch.

It was now early evening and although she was many miles from London, the scene that confronted her was similar to the ones she had faced many times in Regent's or Hyde Park. Various young couples were locked in passionate embraces in the grass and other women, with painted faces, were parading up and down trying to get the attention of one of the many passing soldiers. She noticed a group of young girls giggling and pointing. Edith had also spotted them and marched over.

"Now come along, girls," she said in a firm but motherly tone. "I know it's very exciting seeing all these handsome young men in uniform, but you should really be at home by now. It's teatime and your parents will be waiting. We don't want them to come looking for you now, do we?"

The girls scurried away and Edith peered beneath the rhododendron bush they had been standing next to. Dorothy squinted. She could see a pair of boots and red buckled shoes peeping out.

"Martin Dewhurst, is that you down there?" she heard Edith enquire loudly. "Button up your trousers at once."

The bush shook violently, before a red-faced young couple appeared and hurried away as quickly as the schoolgirls. Dorothy had to stop herself laughing out loud. Edith then made her way towards the nearest bench where a couple were intimately entwined. She tapped the soldier on the shoulder. He looked up and around in anger, then surprise when he saw Edith standing there with her hands on her hips.

"Corporal, you clearly have very deep feelings for this young lady, I am sure you don't want to damage her reputation. Why not spend your evening together at the Temperance Hall dance?" she said handing him a folded pamphlet she produced from her pocket.

Muttering his thanks, the young soldier stood up and led his girlfriend out of the park. Edith continued on her way, with Dorothy staying several steps behind. She was amused and impressed in equal measure.

"George Murton," said Edith to a man with a young lady on each arm, "I pulled you kicking and screaming into this world, now don't make me pull you kicking and screaming out of this park."

Then a little farther along the path, she stopped in front of two prostitutes plying their trade.

"Good evening, ladies. I believe you are new to the town, but I think you have outstayed your welcome. Perhaps you could find your way back to the station before a police van is sent to escort you there instead."

Dorothy could hardly wait to write to Nina and tell her everything she had witnessed. No wonder Chief Constable Casburn had issued her with a warrant card. Edith was doing the work of several constables yet without having made one arrest. Within twenty minutes of her arrival the park was clear except for one older lady slumped on a bench. Edith bent down and gently shook the snoring woman. As she did so an empty bottle of gin rolled out from beneath her skirts. Edith tutted under her breath.

"Come along now, Sheila, that money the army sends home to you while Frank's away isn't to be spent on drink. I know you must miss him, but this isn't the answer. Come on, let's get you home."

Sheila remained comatose, so Edith draped her arm over her shoulders and attempted to hoist her up.

Dorothy hurried over. "Hello, do you need a hand?" she asked as she helped to steady the swaying Sheila.

Edith looked up in surprise. "Thanks, yes. She's heavier than she looks. Honestly, I don't know what's got into everyone these days, to start behaving like this. Everyone's morals seem to have flown out of the window. This park was once a haven of peace for the town. Little children could play here and elderly couples walked arm in arm while the brass band played, but now it's more like Sodom and Gomorrah."

"It's the war I suppose," replied Dorothy. "People don't think the same rules apply anymore."

"Well really, that's no excuse," tutted Edith.

Dorothy moved to Sheila's other side, taking some of the

weight, and together the two women half carried, half dragged their charge out of the park.

"I'm Dorothy Peto, by the way. I'm from the Women Police Volunteers," she explained, a little breathlessly.

"Did Miss Boyle send you? I wrote to her. A lovely lady. She said I could write to her if I ever needed advice."

"Actually, it was Miss Damer Dawson who sent me to help you, but I have to say you are doing rather beautifully yourself."

Edith smiled self-consciously. "I just use my common sense, Miss Peto. It's a pity others can't do the same. Since they turned Belton Park into an army camp some of the town's young women have got quite silly at the sight of all these young men in uniform."

"Belton Park?" asked Dorothy remembering that was the name of the camp Captain Boyle had said he and Lieutenant Gaskill were at before they left for the front. "Is that close to here?"

"Yes, dear. It's less than a mile away."

Dorothy smiled to herself. Being sent away by Mary and Margaret might actually be a blessing in disguise.

Chapter Thirteen

TOGETHER THE TWO of them staggered down the road to take their charge safely home. Edith knocked on the door of a neat little terraced house. It was opened by an elderly woman, who turned out to be Sheila's mother-in-law.

"Not again!" was her only response when she saw the three of them on the doorstep. Accompanied by much haranguing from the old lady, Dorothy and Edith struggled up the stairs and finally deposited the still semi-conscious Sheila in her own bed. Edith made sure she was lying on her side and instructed her mother-in-law to keep checking on her, then the two of them quickly left.

"Well, I think we could both do with a cup of tea after that," said Edith breathlessly as they stepped outside. "Come along, I live on the next street." She led Dorothy down the cobbled path and round the corner to another terrace of small, neat houses. Dorothy followed her through her front door. Edith's house was in darkness, except for a few embers still glowing in the hearth of the front room. Edith raked them over and shovelled on some small lumps of coal from out of the scuttle. Then she lit the oil lamp in the middle of the table and put the kettle on to boil over the fire. Dorothy's offer to help was waved away and instead she was instructed to take a seat at the small round table in the middle of the room. This at least gave her a chance to study her hostess's surroundings.

The room was spotlessly clean and tidy. There was an armchair by the fire with a crocheted blanket folded on the seat and the mantelpiece was covered with photographs of people she assumed were Edith's family. It reminded her a little of Mr Pearson's office. She leant forward to take a closer look at the picture in the centre of the collection. It was of a much younger Edith on her wedding day, with a happy but shy-looking groom.

"That's me and my Bill. It's seven years since I lost him, but sometimes it still feels like only yesterday," explained Edith as she bustled back into the room and placed two cups and saucers on the table along with a plate holding thick slices of bread and butter.

"I'm sorry," replied Dorothy.

"Don't be. I was luckier than many. Our marriage was a happy one, full of fun and laughter. Bill used to tease me that as I'd been born a Smith, I'd only married him so I didn't have to go to the bother of changing my name." She chuckled. "He was always teasing me and the children. We were blessed with three daughters and a son: Francis, Victorine, Annette and James." She handed Dorothy a photograph of the four children, their young faces smiling awkwardly for the camera.

"After Bill died, I had to return to nursing. I couldn't earn a living and look after the children, so my family helped out. Francis and Vicky went back to Birkenhead to be with my parents, while little Annie and James went down to

London to live with their great-aunt. When they first went, I used to forget and would find myself setting extra places at the table, or sometimes I would hear small feet running in the street outside and I would stop to listen in case it was the children hurrying home." She shook her head. "Silly fool!"

Dorothy felt terribly sorry for the older woman as she listened to her chattering away. Unlike many of her fellow volunteers back in London, Edith was not independently wealthy. Far from it. She was a working widow who when war broke out had tried to balance her police volunteering with her job as matron at the local maternity hospital. Now she was attested and receiving a constable's wage she could at least afford to fully devote her time to her police work.

"May I see it? Your warrant card I mean?" asked Dorothy a little shyly. Edith put her hand in her pocket and proudly produced the small square piece of card bearing the Grantham Borough Police crest, along with Edith's name and the signature of Chief Constable Casburn.

"It's rather a pity you have to carry it with you. I should want to frame it and hang it on the wall. How many people have you actually arrested?"

"None. And I don't intend to," she replied briskly, "but at least I will be able to caution the girls I speak to, and it will make them take me seriously. Before they knew I couldn't really do anything."

"Your children must be very proud of you," said Dorothy gently nodding towards the photographs. "Their mother, the first woman to be given the power to arrest."

Edith shrugged as she topped up their cups. "It's a while since I've seen any of them, but they write every Sunday.

What about your family? How do they feel about you being a police volunteer?"

"I think they were a little shocked at first. They thought I wanted to be a writer, but now I can't imagine not being involved with the police. I love the feeling that I have made a difference to other people's lives and it's so interesting. Once, I found a woman's body during a Zeppelin raid and helped investigate her death. I started to think, and I know this sounds silly, but I started to think that once people had got used to the idea of seeing women in police uniform, I might be able to join the regular police as a detective."

Dorothy felt herself flush. Nina was the only other person she'd shared this secret hope with.

Edith smiled at her. "That doesn't sound silly at all. Look at me. This time last year, we were told women would never be attested."

"Yes, but you are the picture of calm and capability. I made rather a fool of myself recently."

"Why do you say that?"

Dorothy took a sip of her tea then began to explain all about the case, what had happened when she'd spoken to Eric alone, and how Inspector Derwent had reacted.

Edith listened carefully without interrupting and reached over to pat her hand when she had finished.

"Don't be so hard on yourself. Everyone makes mistakes. That's how we learn. That's what I always told the young nurses in my charge."

"I'm not sure Inspector Derwent sees it that way. He seemed to think I had jeopardised the whole operation."

"Not at all. I think he trusts your instincts, and it sounds like he may even share them, but a man with his experience knows it's not enough. He knows he must find enough evidence to build a case that will stand up in court when it goes before a wily lawyer like this Eric Curtis fellow you spoke to."

"I hope you're right," said Dorothy feeling slightly mollified.

"From what you have told me it sounds like he's trying to train you up. Getting you to take notes, explaining about motive and opportunity, allowing you to speak to witnesses alone, even making you walk to Battersea when you could have taken a car, seeing for himself if you were up to being on your feet all day like one of his detectives."

"Do you really think so?" she asked. Although she knew he was eager to find a motive for the crime, she had never considered what the motive behind the inspector's own actions might be.

"I do," replied the older woman firmly, "but if I am wrong, you mustn't lose heart. Us women are always too hard on ourselves. You are young and women of your generation will have more opportunities than mine. You mark my words. I went from nursing to policing; you could do the reverse. You arc much younger than me. You seem fit and healthy, and you must have the stomach for it. From what you've told me, you've come across two dead bodies and not been put off policing. There is certainly a call for young women to join the profession both here and at the front. Why not discuss it with Miss Boyle? She seems like a woman full of good ideas."

"She is, but unfortunately she has left the country. She

has gone to Serbia, to be a nurse, as it happens. Like you she had serious misgivings about the Defence of the Realm Act. Rather than enforce the new rules, she resigned her position."

Edith's shoulders slumped. "Oh, I am sorry to hear that. Does that mean Miss Damer Dawson supports the act?"

"She believes in keeping her promise to Sir Edward Henry. She told him we would work to uphold all the laws of the land while our country was at war. How do you feel about DORA?"

"It doesn't sit right with me, threatening to introduce curfews or telling women they can't go into a pub—not that I would want to. The next thing you know, they'll be bringing back the Contagious Diseases Act, forcing women to be medically examined. The horror stories I heard from some of the older nurses at the asylum…"

"The asylum?"

"When I was training to be a nurse, I worked in an asylum that treated patients in the last stages of syphilis. General paralysis of the insane, they used to call it. I saw first-hand the suffering and misery it caused, not just the physical decline and the blindness, but the slow descent into madness of the patients. Poor souls. So you see, Miss Peto, I know more than most how terrible venereal disease is. That's why I volunteered for the police in the first place. I feared an outbreak of that terrible disease in this town with the increase in soldiers and then prostitutes, but I don't think all the blame for it spreading should be put on the women."

"Do you feel strongly enough to resign your position?" asked Dorothy bluntly. This was after all what she had been sent to find out.

Edith looked up in surprise and shook her head. "No, I do not. For one, I can't afford to. The police pay me twenty-eight shillings a week and if I left, there's no saying the Lindis—the hospital where I used to work—would take me back. And for another thing, I understand what Miss Damer Dawson means. I made an oath when I was attested. Put my hand on a Bible and swore in front of the chief constable: 'I do solemnly and sincerely declare and affirm that I will well and truly serve His Majesty, the king, in the office of constable, without fear or affection…' Well, you don't need to hear the rest." She took another sip of tea and sighed. "As usual, we shall just have to try to find a way of working around these new regulations the men have come up with."

They sat in companionable silence for a few minutes listening to the mantelpiece clock softly ticking. Dorothy looked at Edith's wedding photograph again and suddenly remembered something.

"Edith, I don't suppose you know a young woman called Jessica? I don't know her previous surname, I'm afraid, but I understand she recently married a man called Paul Gaskill."

Edith's face clouded. "Married and widowed within the week," she said sadly. "Her husband was a lieutenant who trained at Belton Park before he went to the front."

"Yes, that's right," replied Dorothy eagerly. "Do you know her?"

"Jessica is a nurse at the Lindis, where I used to be a matron."

"Would I be able to meet her, do you think? It was Paul's grandfather, Hector…well it was his murder I was helping to investigate when I spoke to Eric Curtis."

"Good heavens. The grandfather murdered and Paul killed by the Huns. Whatever could one family have done to deserve that? Don't worry, I'll take you to the hospital tomorrow to meet Jessica. Now, it's getting late. Let's get you back to your hotel, Dorothy."

Edith drank down the last few remaining drops of tea. She licked her fingers to extinguish the wick in the lamp and pulled on her jacket. Dorothy followed her outside. It had grown dark while they had been chatting and she was pleased to have someone guide her through the unfamiliar town. As the two of them navigated the dimly lit cobbled streets several army trucks rumbled by.

"More new recruits on their way to the training camp," said Edith shaking her head. "When I first arrived here, Grantham was so friendly and peaceful. Now, thanks to the army taking over Belton Park and soldiers streaming in from all over the country, this little market town has almost doubled in size and is getting as rowdy as Liverpool."

They turned a corner and paused beneath a streetlamp. Across the road there was some sort of commotion going on outside a pub called The Blue Pig. A large group of soldiers and several gaudily dressed women seemed to be having an argument.

"Heavens! What do you think is going on?" asked Dorothy.

Edith felt in her coat pocket for her spectacles. She placed them on her nose and squinted. "I have no idea. I don't recognise anyone. The town is full of strangers these days—so many new faces appearing everywhere. Aren't two of those women the ones I told to leave the park?"

Before Dorothy could answer her, there was a sudden clatter of hooves and wheels on the cobbles, followed by more shouting as a van raced around the corner and stopped abruptly outside the pub. Dorothy glanced nervously at Edith, who was watching silently as about half a dozen men jumped down. They grabbed the three women and roughly dragged them into the back of the van. The women were all kicking and screaming in protest.

"Do you know those officers? Can't we do something?" asked Dorothy urgently.

Edith shook her head. "No. Look at their uniforms. They are military police."

One of the military police officers, a sergeant judging by his stripes, spotted Edith and Dorothy across the street and came marching over.

"Good evening, ladies. It is late for you to be out. Is anything amiss?" he asked as he straightened his cap. He was still a little breathless from struggling with the women.

"Good evening, Sergeant, all is well thank you," Edith replied with a smile, then nodded towards the pub. "By the look of things you and your colleagues are having a busy evening. May we be of assistance? I am Constable Smith and this Miss Peto of the Women Police Volunteers."

The sergeant smirked as he puffed out his chest. "Thank you, ladies, but it is nothing for you to worry your heads about. Just a spot of trouble. It'll all be taken care of very soon."

"And those women, who are they? What are they to be charged with?" asked Dorothy.

"I'm afraid to say, miss, that they are women of the worst class. Since the army took over Belton Park, trainloads of these sorts of women have been arriving along with all the soldiers. They are all here trying to tempt our brave boys with their loose morals."

Another group of soldiers staggered out of the pub, singing raucously. They joined their comrades and began laughing and pointing, as the skirt of one of the women, struggling with the police, rode up above her knees exposing several inches of bare white skin.

"Those soldiers don't look like they need much tempting. They were being just as loud as the women. Why aren't they under arrest too?" asked Dorothy.

The sergeant shook his head and laughed as if she had told a joke.

"Well, you see, miss, it's not that simple. There's hundreds if not thousands of them soldiers all wanting to let off a bit of steam before they are sent overseas, and we're overstretched as it is. It's better all round if we tackle the root of the problem."

"I see." Edith nodded. "The root being these women and their loose morals." She and Dorothy exchanged a glance, but her sarcasm was lost on the young sergeant.

"Precisely, Mrs Smith," he replied, his face breaking into a smile, "and you can be assured we will make your streets safe again, but in the meantime, I must recommend you two ladies don't go out after dark without a chaperone."

With that he strutted back to his comrades and the two women could only watch as the prostitutes in the back of the van were driven away.

"And there we have it. DORA in action," tutted Edith. "No wonder Miss Boyle left the country."

After Edith had safely returned her to the Angel and Royal, Dorothy dined in the hotel restaurant. It wasn't a particularly pleasurable experience and she had little appetite. The food was adequate, but from the sidelong looks of the waitresses and other diners, it was clear they thought a young woman in a strange uniform, dining alone, was rather odd. By the end of the meal, Dorothy felt like an exhibit in a freak show.

Before going up to her room, she used the public telephone at the hotel reception to call Inspector Derwent. Despite the hour, she knew he often worked late into the evening. She wanted to let him know that she had found Jessica, in the hope of making amends for speaking to Eric Curtis without permission.

"Hello, Miss Peto, is that you?" His voice crackled down the line.

She jammed a finger in her free ear to drown out the noise coming from the army officers drinking in the hotel bar as the operator finally put her through. "Yes. Good evening, Inspector."

"The operator told me this call is coming from Grantham."

"That's right."

"What on earth are you doing there?"

"Margaret and Mary sent me up here to meet Edith Smith."

"The woman who has been attested?"

"Yes, but there's more. Belton Park, the camp where Paul

Gaskill was training, is nearby and Jessica, the girl he married, is here too. I'm meeting her tomorrow."

"Miss Peto, we don't know for certain that the marriage took place or if it did that it was legal. Nor do we know anything about this young woman or her background or her family."

"What does her family matter?"

Despite the terrible line, she could still hear him sighing heavily.

"Firstly, if she were from a respectable family, I assume the wedding would not have allowed to be a clandestine affair. They would have wanted it to be announced in *The Times* and so forth. Secondly, if her family is not respectable then perhaps one of their number, hearing of Hector Gaskill's wealth, had the idea of hastening Paul's and therefore Jessica's inheritance. Thirdly, if that is the case, then you may be in danger. They won't take kindly to a young lady from London poking her nose in."

Dorothy bridled at this last comment. "I am doing no such thing. Margaret and I found Hector's body and it would be quite wrong if I did not offer my condolences to his grandson's widow. Good evening, Inspector."

With that she slammed the receiver back in its cradle. So much for making amends. She could just imagine the expression of weary resignation he would be wearing. There was a small cough behind her. She turned and saw the hotel manager with an oil lamp in his hand.

"Perhaps you would like this to help light your way to your room, miss. Coming here all the way from London, you must be overly tired."

Dorothy took the lamp without a word and climbed up the dimly lit staircase. As she lay in the unfamiliar, slightly lumpy bed, Dorothy thought about Edith. Although she had been sent to offer her advice, she had found she was the one learning from the stories the older woman was telling her. She had been as impressed as Nina had been with her fortitude and no-nonsense approach to the difficulties her town was facing and with the way she had spoken bluntly about her concern that the increase in prostitution would inevitably lead to the spread of venereal diseases, through the local population as well as the troops. The way she described her experiences treating those suffering from syphilis when she was training as a young nurse had made Dorothy shudder and, when she closed her eyes, images of the evening began to dance through her mind.

She remembered the obscene shouts of the soldiers as they pointed and jeered. Then the flushed and contorted faces of the women, their makeup smudged and their hair a mess, as they were thrown into the police van.

Chapter Fourteen

THE NEXT MORNING, Dorothy had arranged to meet Edith, who had agreed to take her to meet Jessica Gaskill. They arrived at the Lindis nursing home a little after nine o'clock. The Lindis was the town's only maternity hospital. Dorothy waited near the reception desk while Edith went to enquire about Jessica. There was a strong smell of disinfectant, but the place had a serene feel to it. Nurses with their white caps tied at the napes of their necks spoke in hushed tones as they went about their business calmly and efficiently. After a few moments, Edith returned.

"Jessica isn't working today. She's over in the nurses' home. I've sent a message, asking her to come and meet us here," she explained.

"Is that where she lives, in the nurses' home?" asked Dorothy, but Edith didn't reply. She was distracted, watching a young nurse escorting two women, one with a badly bruised face, to the entrance of the hospital.

When they'd left, she called out, "Nurse Cooper, may I speak with you for a moment, please."

The young nurse stopped abruptly and came towards them with a pale and slightly anxious face. "Yes, Matron?" she asked, nervously.

Edith patted her on the arm. "I've told you, Peggy, you don't need to call me that anymore. I'm Constable Smith now. Those two young women you were talking to at the door, I didn't recognise either of them. Are they from Grantham?"

"No, Matron, I mean, Constable. They are from Nottingham. I think they only arrived here a few weeks ago." She paused for a second. "I think they are here to, you know, to entertain the troops."

"I see, and why are they here at the hospital? Are they pregnant?"

Nurse Cooper shook her head. "No. One had been feeling unwell. I examined her briefly. She had a rash on her palms and white patches inside her mouth."

Edith nodded and turned to Dorothy. "The classic early symptoms of syphilis."

"She didn't want to go to the infirmary. I told her she could stay here and see a doctor, but she wouldn't wait," continued Nurse Cooper.

"And her friend? Did she have similar symptoms?" asked Edith.

"No, but she had a swollen and bruised eye and a badly cut lip. She wouldn't say what had happened though."

"I think we can guess," muttered Dorothy. The other two women nodded silently. Like Dorothy, they had both come across plenty of prostitutes who had suffered when a disgruntled customer had been free with his fists.

"Did they give their names and addresses before they left?" asked Edith.

"Yes. Of course the names may be false, but the address

was genuine. They are both residing at the same house on Millard's Place, Matron," replied the young nurse, who seemed unable to break the habit of addressing Edith that way.

"Maggie Boswell's establishment?" Edith asked.

The nurse nodded.

"I see. Thank you, Nurse Cooper, you may go."

The young girl scurried away.

"Who is Maggie Boswell?" enquired Dorothy.

"She runs the only brothel in the town. With all these soldiers arriving, she must be doing a roaring trade. It certainly seems that she is too busy to check if her girls are safe and healthy. If today's patient really did have syphilis, she would be the Lindis's third case in as many weeks. Heaven knows how many more are out there that we don't know about."

"No wonder the army and politicians are so worried," agreed Dorothy.

"Then they should be providing proper medical care and prophylactics."

At that moment, a tall, slim, fair-haired young woman walked through the entrance.

Edith smiled as soon as she saw her. "Ah, Nurse Swan, there you are. Come and meet Miss Peto. She would like to speak with you. Why don't the two of you chat in my old office," suggested Edith, leading them down a corridor. "They haven't appointed my replacement as yet."

As Edith showed the two women into a small sparsely furnished office, Dorothy had the chance to study Jessica. The name Swan suited her. She was very pretty with a natural elegance and grace about her. Although she seemed composed as she smiled and shook Dorothy's hand, her eyes were wide and staring. They reminded Dorothy of some of the invalided troops returning from the trenches. When she'd asked one of the stretcher-bearers at the station what was wrong with them, he'd told her they were in shock from being shelled day and night by the Germans.

"Why did Edith introduce you as Nurse Swan and not Nurse Gaskill?" asked Dorothy as the two of them sat on either side of the desk and their hostess left, closing the door behind her.

"That was my maiden name. Only a few people know about my marriage. I'd like it to remain that way, at least for the time being. I'm not sure how it could affect my position here. Edith is the only person connected to the hospital who knows. She was my witness."

Dorothy tried not to look surprised. Edith had not mentioned that she had actually attended the wedding.

"I'm terribly sorry about what happened to your husband," she said gently.

"Thank you. It's so strange. I hadn't even got used to calling him that. How did you know we were married? Did you know Paul? Is that why you are here?"

"No, I never had the pleasure of meeting him, but I heard about your marriage from Captain Boyle."

Jessica smiled. "He was Paul's witness. Such a kind man. I received a letter from him only this morning. He wanted me to know that Paul didn't suffer at all."

Dorothy hesitated. "I'm afraid I'm here to relay more bad news. Paul's grandfather, Hector Gaskill, has been murdered."

Jessica's hand flew to her mouth. "Oh my goodness! Murdered! How awful. I had no idea."

"Well as you said, not many of Paul's friends and relatives knew about you."

"When did this happen?"

"Late last Saturday or possibly very early on Sunday morning. A friend of mine is his neighbour. She found his body."

"How awful," repeated Jessica. "I never met him of course, but Paul spoke of him often. He wrote to him to tell him about our marriage. He didn't think he'd approve, but he wanted to try to explain…" She trailed off.

"Is that why you had such a quiet wedding? So, Hector couldn't object?"

A pink flush crept up Jessica's pale complexion and she stared down at her hands. Dorothy noticed she wasn't wearing a wedding band.

"Partly," she said quietly. "I mean we always planned to marry. Paul proposed a week after we met." She smiled to herself at the memory. "He said he knew straight away. I felt the same. From the first second I saw him, I knew he was the one for me. He rode past me on a beautiful chestnut mare and smiled at me as I was walking to work one morning. Then he drove here with a corporal who had been injured during training and needed his hand stitched; it was quicker than going to the infirmary. We agreed to wait until this ghastly war was over. I was going to follow him to the front and take up a position in one of the field hospitals; only…well you see, I discovered I was pregnant." She looked up at Dorothy. "Please don't think badly of me, Miss Peto.

The night Paul came to tell me he was leaving, I'm afraid our emotions rather got the better of us. As it turned out, his leaving was delayed but the deed was done. When I told him, he insisted we marry as soon as possible. I was worried he might be angry, but he was so happy and excited."

Jessica's hands instinctively went to her still-flat stomach and Dorothy's heart went out to the young woman, while her head began whirling through what this might mean for the murder investigation.

"How will you manage? Do you have family who will help care for you?" she asked.

Jessica shook her head. "No, my parents were missionaries. They died out in Africa when I was quite young. I was raised by my mother's sister, but she died two years ago. Auntie Hilda had worked in service. As a housekeeper. It was a very respectable position, but Paul knew his grandfather would simply see me as the girl of a servant. Paul didn't care about things like that. He understood how it felt to be alone in the world, he'd lost his parents when he was young too. He loved his grandfather, but I got the impression he wasn't a warm man." She shrugged her shoulders. "I really don't know what I'll do. Edith thinks I might be entitled to a pension from the army, but when the hospital board finds out I'm pregnant, I will lose my job. Apart from Edith, nobody even knows I am married. I daren't wear my ring."

She carefully showed Dorothy a delicate silver chain she was wearing around her neck hidden beneath her clothes. Dangling on the end was a thin gold band.

"It's very pretty," said Dorothy. "I apologise if this is an indelicate question, but did Paul make a will before he left for France?"

"Yes. All the soldiers were told to. I have it in my room along with our marriage certificate. He left everything to me, not that he had much. There was an allowance from his grandfather. I don't know what will happen about that now."

"Hector was in the process of changing his will when he was killed. He was leaving everything to Paul."

Jessica looked confused. "That's odd. Paul thought his grandfather would disinherit him on the spot. Do you know if he received Paul's letter?"

"He definitely received the letter. The servants recognised Paul's handwriting. According to them, he read the letter, burnt it, then sent for his solicitor."

"That doesn't make much sense."

"Quite a lot about his death doesn't make much sense, I'm afraid," agreed Dorothy.

"Hector's death must have been an awful shock for the servants. Paul told me that the butler and cook had worked for his grandfather for as long as he could remember. Will they be taken care of, do you know?"

"I don't I'm afraid," replied Dorothy. She was struck by the fact that Jessica was the only person connected to the case who had shown any concern for the servants, even though she had never met any of them.

"Did Paul ever talk about Emily or Gerald?" she asked.

Jessica nodded. "Sometimes. He was fond of Emily and felt rather sorry for her. As for Gerald..." She shook her head. "Well from what Paul said, he sounded rather a cad, but Paul said he was harmless enough. Paul always saw the best in people."

Dorothy left Jessica with a promise that she would see if Arnold Pearson could help her in any way. Strangely, there was no sign of Edith anywhere, so she decided to return to her hotel alone. Despite her disappointing conversation with Inspector Derwent the previous evening, she decided she should still inform him that Jessica was indeed Paul's wife, perfectly respectable and pregnant.

After waiting for what felt like an eternity the operator finally put her through to Scotland Yard. She was told that the inspector was away from his office on urgent business. She asked the grumpy-sounding sergeant if she could leave a message, but the crackling line made it so difficult that he finally shouted, "It might be better if you try again at another time, miss. Or better still, send the inspector a telegram."

Dorothy replaced the receiver and was wondering what to do next when she spotted Edith marching past the hotel window. She hurried outside and caught up with the older woman who seemed pleased to see her.

"Oh hello there. How was your meeting with Jessica? Sorry if I abandoned you at the hospital, but after what Nurse Cooper told me, I thought the time had come to deal with Maggie Boswell myself," she said, pointing to the wicker shopping basket she was carrying. It held several odd-shaped packages wrapped in brown paper.

"What do you have there?" enquired Dorothy.

"Supplies from the hospital store cupboard. Maggie Boswell has been a thorn in the side of this town for long enough. Even before war broke out and I began my voluntary patrols, I used to complain to the police about her. I told them bluntly that some of her girls were suffering from venereal diseases and were a danger to themselves and the men who visited them, but the desk sergeant I spoke to always had some excuse or other for doing nothing. Firstly, it was a public health, not a police matter, then they said they were understaffed with so many of their number joining the army, then they finally admitted that they thought it was better to have places like Maggie's, as it kept the women off the streets." She shook her head. "They used to tell me to get myself home, 'make a nice cup of tea, put your feet up and forget all about this nasty business'. Now look what's happened! It's women like Maggie Boswell who have given the politicians an excuse to pass DORA and put the liberties of all women at risk."

"So what do you propose to do now?" asked Dorothy.

"Now we must take matters into our own hands," replied Edith firmly and Dorothy found herself following meekly after the older woman.

Even if she hadn't been with Edith, Dorothy could have guessed which house belonged to Maggie Boswell. It was the only one in the street with the noise of a loud, jangling piano and raucous laughter echoing out of it. They stopped outside and Edith rapped sharply on the door. After a few moments, it was opened by a woman with artificially brassy-blonde hair and overly rouged lips and cheeks. Dorothy knew at once that this must be the notorious Maggie Boswell. She gave a small cough as the strong smell of cheap perfume almost overwhelmed her.

"Edith Smith! Well, to what do I owe this honour?" Maggie asked in a mocking tone.

"Good afternoon, Maggie," replied Edith. "It's very simple. I want you to send the girls you have working here back to Nottingham, or wherever else they've come from."

Maggie laughed out loud as she leant against the door frame and folded her arms across her ample chest. "And I want you and your friend in your silly costumes to get off my doorstep and stop being bloody busybodies, but I expect we'll both we disappointed."

Edith drew herself up to her full height and looked Maggie steadily in the eye but kept her voice low. "I'm here to tell you some of your girls are infected with syphilis. You aren't keeping them clean or safe here. For weeks now they have been coming to the hospital for treatment." She reached into her basket and produced a large brown paper bag. She thrust it towards Maggie. "I have here some prophylactics from the hospital. You need to make sure your clients use them. When venereal disease spreads, it's always the women who bear the brunt. You owe it to the women of this town, your girls and the soldiers they go with to…"

Maggie stopped her before she could say more. She stepped out on to the doorstep, threw the bag to the ground and pointed a scarlet talon in Edith's face. "And I'm here to tell you I don't owe anybody anything," she hissed. "This is my house and I'll run it however I see fit. Now bugger off back to your nursing home and let me get back to work."

With that she turned on her heel and slammed the door in Edith's and Dorothy's faces. Dorothy began scooping up the prophylactics, while Edith placed her basket down and took out two more items: a tin of red paint and a small paintbrush. Dorothy watched in astonishment as she quickly and quietly painted a large crimson V and a D on Maggie's white front door.

"Oh my goodness," murmured Dorothy, feeling a mixture of shock and admiration. It was like being back with Nina, in the days when they were campaigning for the vote, although neither of them had done anything so dramatic when wearing their uniforms. When Edith had finished, she calmly packed her things away and beckoned to Dorothy to follow her. They passed a group of neighbours, who had congregated outside to snigger at Edith's handiwork.

A few seconds later, Maggie's shrill voice could be heard screeching down the street after them. "How dare you, Edith Smith! Who the hell do you think you are? You get back here right now and clean off this muck!" she screamed. Maggie continued to threaten and curse, but Edith just walked with a small, satisfied smile.

"Good heavens, Edith," whispered Dorothy as she trotted after her new friend. "Aren't you worried? She might accuse you of criminal damage."

Edith looked at Dorothy's concerned face and grinned. "No, she won't, and it will wash off eventually. Besides the military police would have caused more damage if they had raided the place. I see it more as, now what did Miss Boyle and the other suffragettes call it? Direct action? It isn't much, but it might make men think twice before knocking on her door."

Chapter Fifteen

DOROTHY WAS RATHER sorry to leave Grantham. She had enjoyed meeting Edith. She'd reminded her of why she and Nina had worked so hard to form the WPV. Part of her wanted to stay in the small northern town rather than return to London, where everything had become so political and unfriendly, but at least if she was back in London, she might be able to help Jessica. She'd liked the young woman very much and could only begin to imagine what she must be going through. She worried about what the future might hold for both her and her unborn child.

As the train rattled along, she stared out of the window. She also had her own future to consider. Was it even in London anymore? Might she be more useful in a smaller city or town? She knew Bath well after spending several summers at art school there. Her father had hoped they might discover some hitherto hidden talent. They hadn't. Or Bristol perhaps? Only the other day, she was reading about how the National Council of Women there were asking for more recruits. Bristol wasn't just a busy port, it was also home to factories producing munitions, motorbikes and chocolate, all in their own way essential for the well-being of the troops on the front line and, like other cities, it had seen a dramatic drop in the number of male police officers. Maybe her skills could be put to better use there, away from Mary and Margaret, and it would put a stop to her daydreaming about becoming a Scotland Yard detective one day. After her last two conversations with Inspector Derwent, that was looking more and more unrealistic.

It was late when she returned to her empty flat in Bloomsbury. She changed into her nightgown and went into the small kitchen to heat up some milk. Like Edith's home, her mantelpiece was covered in family photos. Unlike Edith, her family had never been forced to live hundreds of miles apart. In amongst the pictures of her parents, and brothers and sisters, were several photographs of her grandfather. His building company had made a fortune for the family. One image showed him and the other benefactors at the opening of the Lock Hospital, the capital's first voluntary hospital for the treatment of venereal disease. No doubt she would be able to find a position there as a nurse as Edith had suggested. It had been very kind of her to try to reassure her that her generation had more options. Dorothy tried to imagine herself as a nurse for a moment, but it was no good. She wanted to be a policewoman. More than anything. Like Edith, she wanted to be attested.

The next morning, rather than visit the WPS offices to report to Mary and Margaret, she went straight to Scotland Yard. Even if he was still cross with her, she wanted to tell Inspector Derwent, in person, everything she had learnt in Grantham. However, as she hurried through the entrance, she almost bumped into him going the other way.

"Oh hello there, Inspector. I was just coming to see you."

"Then as ever, Miss Peto, your timing is impeccable," he replied raising his hat. As his face was as impossible to read as ever, she couldn't tell if he was being sarcastic.

"I wanted to tell you that I met with Jessica, Paul Gaskill's wife, and she is absolutely charming, perfectly respectable and about two months pregnant."

This piece of information resulted in the inspector raising an eyebrow, but he didn't speak, so Dorothy continued.

"I did try telephoning yesterday, but the sergeant I spoke to said you had been called away on urgent business."

"I apologise, Miss Peto. In your absence, we have been rather busy too."

"Have you arrested Gerald yet?" she asked hopefully.

"No. I was called out because a body was found beneath Albert Bridge early yesterday morning. It was Connie Beal."

Dorothy stared at him in disbelief. "Connie is dead?"

"I'm afraid so, Miss Peto. Killed by a single blow to the head just yards from the gate that leads into the garden of twelve Cheyne Row."

"Who would do such a terrible thing?"

"Almost as important is the question why."

She gave him an enquiring look. "What do you mean?"

"When Willerby came down to look at the body, he managed to extract a fragment of paper that was clutched in the dead girl's hand. He is still analysing it, but it looked very much like the corner of a ten-pound note."

She realised what he was insinuating and shook her head. "You think Connie was blackmailing someone? Surely not. She seemed like such a nice girl," said Dorothy.

"Hmm. A nice girl who lied to us and spent the night

with a young man who was not her husband."

Dorothy opened her mouth to protest, but he held up his hand to silence her.

"Either way we shall soon know the truth. I'm on my way to see Dr Stirk and Willerby now."

"May I be permitted to join you, Inspector?"

He seemed amused at her meekness.

"The visit would not be the same without the pleasure of your company, Miss Peto."

"I might be mistaken, but you look as though you are almost smiling, Inspector."

"Not at all. I was simply struggling to recall if I'd ever before met a young lady who was so eager to visit a morgue."

"Inspector, it may help if you viewed me as a fellow police officer rather than a young lady."

"Then from now on, Miss Peto, I shall endeavour to do so."

They arrived at the morgue a few moments later. Dr Stirk and Willerby were waiting for them.

"Good morning, Inspector, and how lovely to see you again, Miss Peto," said Willerby brightly.

The doctor nodded towards Inspector Derwent but ignored Dorothy completely. His sleeves were rolled up and, as always, he was puffing on his pipe. Behind him, covered by a sheet was what she assumed was Connie. She didn't have to assume for long. With a dramatic flourish, Dr Stirk briefly removed his pipe from his mouth and threw back the sheet revealing Connie's naked body.

"She was killed by a blow to the side of the head. Her skull was fractured. Death would have been almost immediate," he announced gesturing towards Connie's head with the end of his pipe. "I believe the killer used a jagged piece of concrete. I found traces of concrete dust in the wound."

"That would fit. I found several loose pieces of concrete beneath Albert Bridge just at the base of the pier," explained Willerby.

"Did any have traces of blood on them?" asked the inspector.

"No, but the piece used to kill her was probably thrown in the river," replied Willerby.

"Time of death?" asked the inspector.

"I'd say between ten o'clock and two in the morning judging by the progress of the digestion of her evening meal."

"And her body was discovered at five o'clock in the morning," added the inspector.

"Didn't the boat people see or hear anything?" asked Dorothy.

"They'd left," replied the inspector.

"Rather bad luck actually, Miss Peto," explained Willerby. "I inspected the remains of a fire they must have lit on the embankment to cook their supper. They probably left as soon as they put it out at around ten that night, I'd say."

"Perhaps if they'd been there, she might have been safe." Dorothy sighed.

"Far more likely, one of those ne'er-do-wells attacked her," retorted the doctor with a snort. Dorothy took a step forward. Connie's white face was still streaked with dirt from where she must have fallen, and dried blood could be seen in her matted hair. Her lifeless blue eyes stared back at her. The last time she'd seen her she'd been with Jack and had looked so happy and full of life. Instinctively, she reached out and gently closed her eyelids.

"How dare you touch the body without my permission," snapped the doctor immediately, his face full of fury.

"Haven't you finished your examination, Doctor?" enquired the inspector calmly while Dorothy stepped back, stung.

"Yes, but that's hardly the point," complained the doctor, still glaring at Dorothy as he returned to sucking on his pipe.

"What about the fragment of paper she was clutching, Willerby?" asked the inspector, now turning his attention to the young forensic scientist. "Have you found out anything more?"

The young scientist stood up a little straighter and adjusted his spectacles. "Yes, as I suspected, it was definitely the corner of a ten-pound note."

"But it doesn't definitely mean Connie was blackmailing someone," protested Dorothy who hated the way the young woman's character was being called into question as she lay dead in front of them.

"How else would a maid be in possession of that sort of money?" sneered the doctor. "Mark my words, she was involved in illegal doings of some kind. If it wasn't blackmail, it was something worse. A young woman out at that hour without a chaperone. Gentlemen, I trust you understand my meaning?"

He gave the inspector and Willerby a knowing nod. Dorothy understood his meaning too and she was tired of being sidelined.

"When you examined her body, did you find any signs of sexual activity, Doctor?" she asked bluntly.

The doctor's face flushed a dangerous shade of puce as he glowered at her. "I did not." He sucked deeply on his pipe. "But I can tell you she was not a virgin."

Willerby gave a small cough. "I have heard that, well, that could be down to other activities. Horse riding for example or gymnastics or…" He trailed off as Dorothy and the doctor both turned to stare at him. Meanwhile, the inspector was pacing the floor, the tap, tap of his walking stick echoing against the wooden floorboards as he ignored the others' discussion.

"I should have known this would happen. When Connie told us she returned to the house early in the morning but swore she didn't see anything, I should never have believed her. She was a young woman who noticed everything. And that business of hearing whistling." He was talking quietly, as if to himself, but Dorothy replied anyway.

"If you truly believe she was blackmailing the killer, then it doesn't necessarily mean it was her idea. I think someone must have put her up to it, or perhaps she was trying to convince the killer to confess, or perhaps the money was for someone else."

Dorothy knew she was starting to sound desperate, but it was the only way she could believe what the three men seemed convinced was true. Connie had always struck her as someone who had found herself in a difficult situation but who wanted to do the right thing. Had she been wrong about her all along?

The inspector stopped pacing and slowly nodded his head. "Come along, Miss Peto. I want to pay Mrs Platt another visit. My life will be far easier if you act as conduit."

"Haven't you spoken to her since that first morning? After Duckworth said she and Hector Gaskill argued, I would have thought…"

"Yes," interrupted the inspector tetchily. "We tried to speak to her the day before yesterday, but unfortunately a letter from Paul's commanding officer had arrived that morning. In it he expressed his condolences and praised Paul's qualities as both an officer and a gentleman. It seems Gerald had opened it and thrown it away. Mrs Platt found it and read it. She was obviously upset when we arrived, so what with the sobbing and the deafness, we didn't make much progress. Come along, let's not waste any more time. Good day, gentlemen." He raised his hat to Dr Stirk and Willerby before striding out of the room. Dorothy followed him obediently, thinking how typical it was of Gerald to throw away Captain Boyle's letter about Paul.

The inspector was pacing up and down impatiently again while Dorothy sat at the kitchen table holding Mrs Platt's hand. They had taken a taxicab from the morgue to Cheyne Row and the weeping cook had opened the door to them. All she had managed to say so far, was "It's such a terrible shock!", "Poor Connie!" and "Who would do such a thing?" Dorothy suggested she might feel more comfortable talking to them in the kitchen; after all it was her domain, and she made them all a cup of tea while the older lady kept wiping away her tears with a large white handkerchief.

"Did Connie mention meeting anyone when she left the

house the night before last, Mrs Platt?" asked Dorothy as she took a seat at the table opposite the cook. The older woman nodded her head.

"Yes, she was going to meet Jack, her young man, but I didn't know she hadn't come back until I came down this morning and saw the stove hadn't been lit. Next thing, the police are knocking on my door. It was such a terrible shock."

"So, this time she wasn't sneaking out?" asked the inspector in a loud voice.

Mrs Platt looked offended. "Connie didn't sneak, sir. She was a good girl. She really was, and a hard worker too. She told me that Jack had been given leave before going away to training camp and that she was going to meet him. I knew all about it."

Dorothy glanced up at the inspector. "Have you spoken to Jack?"

"No. Sergeant Clark is trying to contact his regiment."

Dorothy nodded and turned her attention back to Mrs Platt. "It must have been strange for the two of you these last few days what with everything that has happened," she said gently.

The cook nodded and fat tears started rolling down her cheeks again. "Oh it has, miss. First, the master and Mr Paul, then Mr Duckworth having to leave. Not to mention Mr Gerald moving in. I said to Connie only yesterday, 'It's never easy getting to know a new master and his ways'." She dabbed at her face with her handkerchief.

"When did you last see him?" asked the inspector.

The cook looked slightly bewildered. "I told the other

policeman this morning, the one in uniform. After dinner we had a bit of a cuddle here in the kitchen. Like I said it had been a trying time and we'd grown quite close." The inspector, who was standing behind the cook raised his eyebrows at Dorothy as Mrs Platt continued to talk. "Then she was off out of the garden door, and I waved her goodbye."

Dorothy tried not to smile, as the inspector silently threw his hands up in despair.

"No, Mrs Platt, not Connie. When did you last see Gerald Gaskill?" she asked, speaking slowly so she could read her lips.

"Mr Gerald? Let me see that was after dinner that night too. I'd made him his favourite: roast lamb. Then he went upstairs to collect his hat and cane. We were clearing the table as he came back down and then he went out for the rest of the evening."

"And he hasn't returned?" asked the inspector who had now positioned himself in front of his witness.

"No, sir. I don't think so. At least I didn't hear him come back and his bed hadn't been slept in."

"Mr Duckworth told us that you and Mr Hector Gaskill argued on the day before we found his body. Is that correct?" asked the inspector.

"Mr Duckworth said what?" The old woman looked confused.

Dorothy moved a little closer to her. "Mrs Platt. Did you and Hector Gaskill argue the day he died? Did he threaten to sack you?"

The cook bowed her head and began crying again. "Yes, he did. It wasn't my fault. He was angry when I asked him for a pay rise. He told me I should be grateful he hadn't sacked me. He said I couldn't hear him ringing the dinner bell. But that only happened once, sir." She looked up at them both with pleading eyes and gestured to the row of bells high on the wall, each labelled with the relevant room or door. "I swear they have got quieter over the years. Normally, Connie or Mr Duckworth is down here to let me know if I miss the dining-room bell. That's the only bell I need to listen out for, you see. Mr Duckworth deals with the front door, the drawing room and the library and Mr Gaskill's room, and Connie sometimes goes, but…"

The inspector was behind Mrs Platt again now and making a winding motion to Dorothy with his hand.

"May I ask why you asked Hector Gaskill for a pay rise?" she interrupted politely.

"I wasn't being greedy, miss, really I wasn't." She paused and loudly blew her nose. "But I have a niece, Ruth, and she has a little baby boy. With him being so young, she can't leave him and go out to work, so I have to help take care of them."

"Doesn't her husband provide for them?" the inspector almost bellowed and Dorothy wished he would leave the questioning to her. If he hadn't been so tetchy during the journey over here, they could have agreed what enquiries they should make. Mrs Platt looked startled at first, then she looked down at her hands resting in her lap and began twisting her own wedding ring.

"She has no husband, sir."

"She's a widow, like yourself?" asked Dorothy.

Mrs Platt looked up. "No, miss. She never married. She's

a good girl, but she was taken advantage of by a young gentleman. A gentleman who should have known better."

"I see. Does this gentleman have a name?" asked the inspector.

"I'm sure he does, sir, but Ruth would never share it. She was always loyal to him, even if he wasn't to her." She cast a suspicious glance at the inspector. "And before anyone should go digging about in my past, I want you to know that I've never been married neither. Platt is the name I was born with, but it wouldn't do for a cook or housekeeper to be known as miss. A woman in my position in a household deserves some respect."

Dorothy nodded, she knew Mrs MacFee, her parents' housekeeper, had never been married either. Then she suddenly recalled something Mary had told her.

"Mrs Platt, did Ruth used to work here before Connie?"

"That's right, miss. I asked Mr Gaskill to give her a job when she came up to London after her father, my brother, died. She was here for nearly two years, and she was a hard worker, but when she started to show, the master dismissed her on the spot."

"And you have been supporting her ever since?"

"Yes, as best I can, miss."

"Just one more question, Mrs Platt. When did your disagreement with Mr Gaskill take place? Was it before or after the letter from Paul arrived?"

"It happened just before, miss. Mr Duckworth knocked on the door and brought it in as I was about to come back down here to the kitchen. Come to think of it he was probably listening at the door. I maybe shouldn't say so, but it seems all these years of working together don't count for much. There's no loyalty in this world." And with that she began sobbing again.

Chapter Sixteen

THEY LET THEMSELVES out of twelve Cheyne Row after Dorothy had made the still-upset Mrs Platt another cup of tea.

"Why did you ask what time Mrs Platt argued with her employer?" enquired the inspector.

"I think we have all assumed it was the arrival of Paul's letter that made Hector cross, but I was wondering if it could have been something else. You remember, Connie mentioned his bad mood when we first spoke to her. She thought it was about the arrival of the barges, but it may have been caused by his disagreement with Mrs Platt, or perhaps he had begun to suspect his butler of twenty years was stealing from him."

He nodded thoughtfully. "Possibly. I agree Paul's letter may not have been the only catalyst that led to him wanting to change his will. At this moment though, I would be more interested to discover the identity of the man who fathered Ruth's child."

"If I were in the habit of gambling, I would put a large sum of money on Gerald being responsible. Mary practically told me so."

"But he wasn't the only male in the household. There

was Duckworth. An older man, in a position of responsibility…"

"Mrs Platt described him as a gentleman. I don't think she would say that about Duckworth if he was responsible," interrupted Dorothy.

"That's true," he conceded, "but it still doesn't necessarily mean it was Gerald. There was Paul, even Hector himself."

Dorothy shook her head firmly. "Not Hector! He was far too old."

The inspector adjusted his necktie a little. "I have heard some young women prefer a more mature man."

"And not Paul surely. Everyone speaks so highly of him."

"I prefer to judge a man on his actions. I hope you will excuse me if I speak plainly, Miss Peto. You told me his wife was already with child when they married, which means he was prepared to take advantage of a young lady out of wedlock. That young lady became pregnant. Perhaps it was a case of history repeating itself." He held up his hand as Dorothy began to protest. "Although, I agree he did marry Jessica. So, while I respect the fact the young man died fighting for our country, it does not make him a saint."

Suddenly a black police car came zooming down the street and stopped with a screech in front of them. The large figure of Sergeant Brook jumped out.

"There you are, sir, Miss Peto. Willerby said you had come here," he said slightly breathlessly. "There's been a development."

"Have you found Gaskill?" asked the inspector.

"No, sir, but Mr Pearson's office has been broken into.

The place has been completely turned over. Whoever did it made a right mess."

"Did they take anything?"

"We don't think so, but Mr Pearson is still checking. It was his clerk who reported it. A sergeant and constable from Holborn arrived first then, when Mr Pearson arrived, he asked them to contact us."

"Then let's get down there," replied the inspector.

The three of them climbed into the car and sped off. Sergeant Taylor was driving and Dorothy couldn't help thinking he enjoyed blasting the horn a little too much as he accelerated through the streets. They arrived outside Mr Pearson's office only ten minutes later. Dorothy stepped out feeling rather shaken and followed the three detectives inside. None of them had asked her to join them, but she hadn't been dismissed either. If she remained quiet and didn't get in the way, they might not even notice she was there.

They passed a uniformed constable standing guard at the entrance and made their way through into the reception area. Then they all paused at the open door that led through into Mr Pearson's office. It was in utter chaos. Plants and photographs had been knocked over, the window was wide open as were all the desk and filing cabinet drawers, and the carpet was covered in letters and other legal documents. Poor Arnold Pearson was standing in the doorway holding his birdcage aloft in one hand, the photograph of Emily in the other and looking even more perplexed than usual. He stepped aside when he heard them arrive.

"Oh hello, Inspector, gentlemen, Miss Peto. They have made such a dreadful mess. Who could want to do such a thing? The birds are terribly upset."

"Has anything been taken?" asked the inspector.

The solicitor shook his head. "We don't think so. Dennis is still checking," he replied nodding towards the elderly clerk, who was on his hands and knees by the filing cabinet retrieving the countless papers strewn across the floor. "Mr Willerby said we could begin tidying up as he couldn't find any fingerprints on the desk or cabinets."

The inspector stepped into the office, carefully making his way across the few exposed pieces of rug. Dorothy and the other detectives followed him.

"You didn't waste any time getting here, Willerby," commented the inspector.

The young scientist, who had been kneeling down with his head out of the window, rose to his feet. "Yes, I bumped into Brook and Taylor as I was heading back to Scotland Yard, so I thought I'd head over and take a look."

"But no fingerprints to be found in here?"

"No, the intruder must have been wearing gloves and the office was cleaned yesterday evening."

"Mrs Parkin is very thorough," chimed in Mr Pearson.

Inspector Derwent nodded to Sergeant Brook and Taylor. "Get her address and go and speak to her. Find out what time she left and if she saw anything."

"I believe her details are through here, gentlemen," said Mr Pearson. The two detectives followed him through into the reception area and the inspector focused his attention back on the scientist.

"So you haven't found anything?"

"Actually, I have. I believe I have found a connection to

the Gaskill case."

The inspector raised an eyebrow. "Are you going to tell me whoever did this was right-handed?"

Willerby grinned. "No, Inspector. In fact, not only am I sure he was left-handed, by the direction he's scattered the files in—you see they have all been pulled out of the drawers and thrown down to the left—but I also know his identity." The young scientist was clearly enjoying himself.

"Are you planning on sharing this information at any point?" asked the inspector, who clearly wasn't.

"It was Duckworth. The butler."

"How do you know?" asked Dorothy not able to keep quiet any longer.

"Well, as I said, whoever broke in here must have been wearing gloves. I couldn't find any prints on the files except those of Mr Pearson and his clerk, but the intruder was careless. He must only have put on his gloves after he had climbed through the window. There is a clear thumbprint on the windowsill. Although I don't have my records with me, I am as certain as I can be that it matches the ones we took of Duckworth when he was arrested."

He beckoned them over to the window and sure enough there was the print. Willerby used the end of the pencil he kept behind his ear to point to a clear straight line going across. "I asked Duckworth about it when his prints were being taken at the station, I was supervising as the custody sergeant hadn't carried out the procedure before," he explained. "And Duckworth told me it was a scar from when he'd cut his thumb when he was a young footman, learning how to use a corkscrew correctly."

"Oh my goodness! How clever of you to remember," declared Dorothy, making the young man blush instantly.

"Not at all, Miss Peto. I paid particular attention to the evidence we collected against Duckworth. At the time of this arrest, we thought he might be Hector Gaskill's killer."

Inspector Derwent cleared his throat, before calling out loudly, "Taylor! Brook! Forget the cleaner for now. Get yourselves down to Hackney. See if Duckworth is still at his sister's pub. If he is, bring him in for questioning."

"Yes, sir," replied the detectives in unison from the outer room followed by the sound of running feet and a door loudly slamming shut.

"Why would Duckworth risk getting into trouble again?" wondered Dorothy out loud.

"He should have been locked up," muttered the inspector.

"Sir, if I may interrupt," said Dennis from his position on the floor. "All the documents in the file assigned to Mr Hector Gaskill have been opened. Not just removed from the drawer, but untied too…" He gestured to the bits of pink tape in amongst the papers.

"What on earth could Hector's butler have been looking for?" asked Mr Pearson who had reappeared in the doorway.

"Is there any document that refers to Mr Duckworth in Hector Gaskill's file?" asked the inspector.

"No. The previous will did and I'm sure Mr Duckworth was aware of that fact. However, as you know, there is no copy of that document."

The inspector nodded. "Perhaps Duckworth wanted to check for himself. Or perhaps somebody sent them to look on their behalf."

"Gerald?" ventured Dorothy.

"I have to say Gerald has been most rude about my professional competence," said Mr Pearson. "He seemed to find it impossible to believe I didn't have a copy of Hector's will, even though he knew better than anyone how difficult his uncle could be."

"When did you last see him?" asked the inspector.

"Oh, a few days ago. We bumped into each other in the foyer of Emily's mansion block. He was arriving as I was leaving. Actually, come to think of it, it was the day you had visited me, Miss Peto. I'd gone to tell Emily about Paul's marriage."

The inspector threw her a questioning look. She didn't want to get into trouble for speaking to witnesses without his permission again, so she quickly asked another question.

"Do you think Connie knew something about what happened here? Is that why she was killed?"

"Could she and Duckworth have been working together?" suggested Willerby.

Dorothy frowned as she tried to imagine this scenario. Inspector Derwent shrugged.

"Hopefully we'll be able to ask him about that when Brook and Taylor bring him in. Willerby, you had better come with me. I want to look at the records to be sure that fingerprint is definitely his. Good day, Mr Pearson, Miss Peto."

And with that the inspector left. Willerby gave Dorothy an apologetic smile as he hurried after him. She watched them go, then bent down and began collecting up the scattered legal papers.

"Let me help you here," she offered.

Mr Pearson beamed at her. "That's very kind, Miss Peto. Thank you."

Dorothy sighed. It looked like she was going to have to wait to hear what the butler had to say and, in the meantime, she was back to filing again.

THAT NIGHT THERE was a heavy thunderstorm. The next morning, Dorothy had to dodge several large puddles on her way to the WPS offices, but at least the storm had finally brought an end to the unbearable oppressive heat.

Unfortunately, the change in weather had done nothing to improve the atmosphere in Little George Street. Dorothy arrived to find Mary in the ante office banging desk drawers open and closed, while Margaret was trying to calm down her dogs who were barking loudly at the noise.

"Where on earth have you been?" complained Mary as soon as Dorothy entered room. "We were expecting you yesterday. I telephoned your hotel in Grantham and they said you had left the day before."

"I'm here now," replied Dorothy removing her hat and coat.

"Just as well. We are expecting twenty new recruits to arrive at any minute. Who would begin their training, if you weren't here? And another thing, their enrolment forms have completely disappeared. How are we meant to register them?"

Dorothy calmly walked over to the filing cabinet, opened the drawer marked 'Recruitment', picked out the correct folder and silently handed it to Mary.

"Thank you, Dorothy. I really don't know what I'd do without you," replied Margaret as Mary stomped out of the room with the folder under her arm.

"Actually, Margaret, I've been considering leaving London. It isn't the same living here with Nina and Raymond both gone. I've been thinking of taking up a paid position, possibly in Bath or Bristol. The NCW are asking for more recruits in both cities."

Margaret's face fell. "Oh, Dorothy, please don't make any rash decisions. I know things here might be a little difficult at times, but think of all the progress we have made. Nobody blinks an eye when they see our members out on patrol and the male police officers have accepted us. Some even appreciate our work."

"I know," conceded Dorothy. "I just seem to spend most of my time on administrative tasks these days. It doesn't feel like I'm making much of a difference."

"That simply isn't true," protested Margaret. "Look how you have been helping Inspector Derwent with poor Mr Gaskill. I know we've asked you to help with the new recruits an awful lot, but that's because you have such a wealth of experience, and you are far more organised than the rest of us. I would be lost without you, so please promise you won't give up on us just yet."

Dorothy smiled. Despite all the recent dramas, she was still very fond of Margaret.

"Very well, Margaret. I promise."

"That's wonderful," replied Margaret clapping her hands together and setting the dogs off barking again. Dorothy collected her notebook and was almost out of the door when she heard Margaret call after her, "Oh and, Dorothy, please don't mention the NCW to Mary. She gets terribly cross about them."

A few moments later, Dorothy found herself addressing twenty eager and expectant faces. They were a group of women aged between twenty-five and forty, all keen to help keep the city safe. Between them Mary and Dorothy took them through basic first aid, self-defence and traffic hand signals. Finally, Dorothy tried to prepare them for what they were most likely to face when on patrol. She explained the best way to deal with problems regarding prostitution, and drunk soldiers and sailors on leave. She told them never to leave a drunkard unattended, and if possible to give them as much black coffee laced with bicarbonate of soda as they could. The new recruits dutifully noted down everything she was saying, and it was only as she watched them fill page after page of their notebooks, that Dorothy realised Margaret was right. She had gained a huge amount of knowledge over the last year, if only she could put it to use a little more often.

AFTER THE TRAINING session had finished, Dorothy hurried out of the offices and took the tube to Battersea. When she'd helped Mr Pearson and his clerk tidy the office, she'd begun to tell him about Jessica being pregnant, which immediately sent him into another panic.

"Good heavens, that complicates things even more. Dear me!" He then went on to suggest they meet again at Emily's flat to discuss the matter in more detail.

"Emily thought of Paul as a brother. I know she will want to help his widow in any way she can," he had declared confidently.

When she arrived at the flat, Dorothy found the two of them waiting for her. Emily led her through to the sitting room where she had a tray of tea, sandwiches and cakes laid out. Mr Pearson was sitting in an armchair with Emily's cat purring contentedly in his lap. As Dorothy settled on to the sofa, Emily began pouring the tea. Dorothy noticed that she wasn't wearing her veil and didn't need to ask Mr Pearson how he took his tea. She simply added four lumps of sugar and stirred it well before handing it to him with a smile. They looked for all the world like a happily married couple.

"Thank you so much for coming, Miss Peto," began Emily. "I must admit I was a little taken aback when Arnold first told be about Paul's wife. I didn't know he even had a sweetheart. Although perhaps it isn't the sort of thing young men discuss. Had they been courting very long?"

"Quite some time, I believe," began Dorothy diplomatically. "They met at the hospital where Jessica is a nurse. They decided to marry before Paul left for the front."

Emily frowned. "Am I to understand she is also with child?"

"That's right," replied Dorothy before taking a quick sip of her tea. Mr Pearson shifted uncomfortably in his seat.

"I don't wish to offend you, Miss Peto," he began cautiously, "but overnight I gave this matter some considerable thought. Are you quite sure the young lady is genuine? She couldn't perhaps be an imposter?"

"Oh, Arnold! Surely not!" gasped Emily.

"I'm sorry, my dear, but these things do happen. A young woman finds herself in trouble and claims to be the widow of a young man who has fallen rather than face the shame of her situation."

Dorothy shook her head. "No, Mr Pearson, I am quite sure everything she told me is true. I've also spoken to both witnesses who were present at the ceremony. One is the town's female police constable and the other is Paul's superior officer, Captain Boyle. He's an acquaintance of mine."

"Then we should thank the Lord for bringing us some good news," replied Emily, clasping her hands together in delight. "I admit I had begun to despair, Miss Peto. So many terrible things were happening. First Uncle Hector, then Paul and poor Connie the maid, then the break-in at Arnold's office, but finally we have something to give us joy. A new life to celebrate. It gives me such comfort to know that Paul and Uncle Hector will live on in their child and great-grandchild, not just in our memories."

She seemed to be quite overcome with emotion. Mr Pearson reached across and patted her arm tenderly.

"Do you know anything of the new Mrs Gaskill's plans, Miss Peto? Will she stay in Grantham? Does she have family there?" he asked while Emily refilled his cup.

"She has no family and I doubt she will be allowed to continue to work at the hospital when her condition becomes obvious," explained Dorothy.

"The poor thing! Is there anything that can be done to help her?" asked Emily.

"I rather hoped you might be able to tell me that," replied Dorothy.

"I'll certainly do all I can, Miss Peto," said Mr Pearson, then he shook his head ruefully. "If Paul had to die, why couldn't it be after Hector? Then this helpless young woman and her child would inherit his estate and their security would be ensured. And why, oh why did I allow myself to be bullied into destroying the first will, without securing a copy of the second one?"

"Now you mustn't blame yourself, Arnold. If Gerald is set to inherit from Uncle Hector, as seems likely, then I am sure we could prevail upon him to assist in some way," began Emily, but Mr Pearson shook his head and patted her arm again. He looked as unconvinced as Dorothy was that Gerald would ever assist anyone but himself.

"Miss Peto, were you able to ascertain if Paul had made a will before he left for the front?" the solicitor asked.

"Yes, he did, and he left everything he owned to Jessica. She has the will in her possession."

"Good. Well, that's something. Paul had some investments—shares and bonds he'd inherited from his parents. Not a huge amount, but still something, as I say. I shall start looking into the matter."

Dorothy smiled with relief. It didn't sound as though Jessica and her child had been left completely destitute after all.

"Miss Peto, I should very much like to write to Jessica

and introduce myself, perhaps even invite her to come and stay here while Arnold sorts out her financial affairs. Would you be kind enough to give me her address?" asked Emily.

"Of course," replied Dorothy. "I'm sure she'd be happy to hear from you."

She followed Emily over to her desk and watched as she carefully copied down the address of the Grantham nurses' home from Dorothy's address book. Then after refusing Emily's offer of a second cup of tea, she made her excuses and left. She had achieved what she had come for: to find Jessica some assistance. And now she wanted to pass on the good news.

She hurried back to Bloomsbury and without even stopping to remove her hat and jacket, she wrote a letter to Jessica herself. She described how keen Emily and Arnold Pearson were to meet her and how they had promised to do all they could to help and that she hoped she didn't mind, but that she had passed her address on to Emily. When she'd finished, she sealed the envelope, found a first-class stamp and dashed down to the post box in the square, just in time to catch the postman picking up the last collection of the day.

Chapter Seventeen

THE NEXT MORNING, Dorothy was on patrol at St Pancras Station, or rather she was supervising two new recruits who were patrolling the station for the first time. She stood some distance away, watching as they confidently spoke to new arrivals who seemed lost and shooed away a group of suspicious-looking boys who were loitering outside the public washrooms. Then, out of the corner of her eye, she caught sight of Sergeants Brook and Taylor. They were leaving the ticket office and making their way across the concourse. She hurried after them.

"Hello there, gentlemen," she called out.

Both men stopped and raised their hats. "Good morning, Miss Peto," replied Taylor, the slightly less taciturn of the two.

"What brings you both here?" she asked, as it was obvious that they weren't going to volunteer the information.

"We are trying to locate Gerald Gaskill, miss."

"Hasn't he returned to Cheyne Row yet? What about Mr Duckworth?"

"We have Duckworth in custody, but Gaskill has disappeared into thin air. We think he may have left London, so we are checking all the stations. Have you seen him, miss?"

"No, I would have telephoned you if I had. Has Duckworth said anything about the break-in at Mr Pearson's office?"

The two detectives exchanged a glance.

"You'd better ask the inspector that, miss."

With that the two detectives tipped their hats to her again and strode away. Dorothy glanced over to her two new recruits. They seemed to be managing perfectly well. She was sure they didn't need her hovering around any longer.

Half an hour later, she arrived at the incident room in Scotland Yard. Inspector Derwent was standing in front of the blackboard. He turned around when she appeared, out of breath and in his doorway.

"Sergeants Taylor and Brook said you were holding Mr Duckworth. Has he said anything about Connie?" she asked immediately.

"Good morning, Miss Peto. No, he did not. He seemed genuinely shocked to hear of her death. In fact, Sergeant Clark followed him when he left here, and he went straight to Westminster Abbey and lit a candle."

"When he left here? You released him? So soon?"

"Yes."

"Why?"

"That was the agreement we came to in return for information about Gerald Gaskill."

"What information?"

"Duckworth admitted breaking into Pearson's office, but he said he did so on the instructions of Gerald Gaskill. Gaskill sought him out in Hackney. He threatened to reconsider making a statement about the theft of the candlestick, if Duckworth didn't do as he said."

"But why did Gerald want anyone to break into Mr Pearson's office?"

"It seems he had become frustrated with the progress or should I say lack of progress Pearson was making in settling Hector's estate. He wanted Duckworth to steal all the relevant papers so he could hand them to a more efficient lawyer. He instructed Duckworth to make such a mess so they might not notice what had been taken at first."

"But nothing was taken."

"No, apparently Duckworth came to his senses. He said it was the tweeting of the birds. He saw them locked up their cage and realised if he was arrested again for theft, he could well find himself behind bars too."

"That's rather poetic."

"I thought it might appeal to you."

Dorothy thought for a moment. "What if Gerald told Duckworth to kill Connie? If he would consider committing one crime for him, why not another? Perhaps he was lighting a candle for his own soul."

"We did think to check his alibi for the time Connie was killed before releasing him, you know, Miss Peto." Dorothy felt herself blush, but he appeared amused rather than cross. "The night she was killed," he continued, "Duckworth was having a lock-in with several acquaintances at his sister's pub. He left at about one o'clock in the morning and went straight to Pearson's office. He told us he needed some Dutch courage. There wouldn't have been time for him to go all the way to Chelsea too."

"So we are back to Gerald again," groaned Dorothy.

"We would be if we could find him, and he isn't the only one we're looking for. The army have been in contact with us. Jack Hurst is absent without leave. The military police are trying to track him down, but they have asked us to inform them if we hear anything."

"Did he run away?"

"Not exactly. He and the rest of his regiment were given twenty-four hours' leave two days ago before they left for a new training camp on the South Coast, as Connie had told Mrs Platt, but he never returned."

Dorothy frowned. "Do you think it's possible he could have killed her?"

"The thought had occurred to me."

"But they were in love. Why would he kill her?"

"Sadly, he wouldn't be the first young man to kill the object of his affections."

Dorothy knew he was right, but she just couldn't imagine it.

"It doesn't make sense though. If he wanted to kill her, he could have taken her somewhere secluded, not attacked her in the open air."

The inspector shrugged. "Perhaps he was going to surprise her, but he caught her with someone else or perhaps they arranged to meet, and they quarrelled. Regrettably, the options are endless."

"What will happen to him if the military police find him?" she asked, unsure if she wanted to hear the answer.

"I expect he'll have to face a court martial."

"And if he's found guilty?"

"At a time of war, desertion is punishable by death, Miss

Peto," he replied and turned his attention back to the blackboard.

Dorothy left Scotland Yard with a head full of questions. Why hadn't Jack returned to his barracks? He must have heard about Connie. Was it simply grief or something more? Despite what the inspector had said, she couldn't bring herself to believe he had killed her. But had he seen her that night? Could he be dead too? No doubt the military police had visited his uncle's house. If he wasn't there, where else could he be? Maybe somewhere he could feel close to Connie.

She arrived at Cheyne Row a little after one o'clock. Instead of going to the front door, she walked round to the garden gate. As she had hoped, it was unlocked. She sneaked through and walked across the garden, keeping close to the wall. When she reached the house, she crept down the steps that led to a small yard and peered through the small kitchen window. She could only see about half of the room. Mrs Platt was putting something in the oven. She was alone, but there were two mugs on the table. Dorothy moved to the door and knocked loudly twice. Nothing. She tried yanking on the doorbell next and heard the loud jangling from inside. Then she knocked again. Finally, the back door opened.

"Oh, Miss Peto, you did give me a fright!" exclaimed the cook clutching at her chest. "I wasn't expecting visitors."

"I'm sorry, Mrs Platt. May I come in?"

"Yes, of course." She stepped to one side and as Dorothy walking into the kitchen she noticed that the two mugs had been moved to the sink. Her eyes scanned the room. The door leading into the pantry was ajar.

"I was just passing and wondered if Gerald had returned home yet? I know the police are still looking for him."

"No, miss," replied the cook. "At least I haven't seen him, but I think he may have been here. When I went to check his room this morning, his overcoat was missing. The one he wears during the day not his evening one."

"Really?" replied Dorothy wondering if the inspector knew this. Perhaps Brook and Taylor were right to think Gerald had left London. "It must be strange to be in this large house all alone," she continued.

The cook flushed and her eyes darted to the pantry door.

Dorothy decided to follow her hunch. "You may as well come out, Jack. I know you're in there."

The door slowly creaked open and out he stepped, unshaven and his uniform crumpled. With his pale face and red-rimmed eyes, he looked like he hadn't slept for days.

"You shouldn't be here, you know. You are going to be in an awful lot of trouble," chided Dorothy gently.

"I told him he should go back but he's been so upset. I said if he explained about Connie, his commanding officer would understand," said Mrs Platt, patting the young man on his arm.

Jack looked down at his feet. "I couldn't concentrate on my training or anything else until I find the animal who killed my Connie. Do you think it was Gerald? Is that why you're here?"

"I don't know," replied Dorothy. "I only know that Inspector Derwent and his men are trying to find him."

Jack curled one hand into a fist and slammed it again his other palm.

"If I find out it was him, I'll kill him."

"Don't talk like that, lad," said Mrs Platt gently. "There's been enough killing."

Jack dropped his head again. "Is there any reason the two of you would suspect Gerald? Had Connie said anything about him?"

Jack turned to Mrs Platt. "Tell her what you told me."

Dorothy looked at the cook expectantly.

The older woman took a deep breath. "I only remembered when Jack and I were talking, but something odd happened on the night Connie was killed. Mr Gerald was going out for the evening, like I told you and the inspector, miss. Well, me and Connie had been clearing the table in the dining room and were walking through the hall as Mr Gerald came down the stairs, puffing on his cigar and whistling away. Then all of a sudden, Connie just froze, like she'd seen a ghost and stared at him."

"Did she say anything?"

"Not a word. After a second, she recovered herself. I asked her if she was all right. She said yes, but she still seemed shaken and asked if she could leave early. She said she'd go to Fulham and meet Jack there. She took her apron off, washed her hands, combed her hair. I gave her a hug and she set off down the garden. She stopped at the top of the steps and gave me a wave." Her lip began to tremble. "And that's the last I saw of her."

Jack put his arm around her. "We had arranged to meet on the King's Road. We were going to go to the music hall," he explained.

"You hadn't arranged to meet by the river?" asked Dorothy with a frown.

"No, miss, on the King's Road. She didn't like going down to the river since we found Mr Gaskill's body," explained Jack. "She didn't even like the garden much anymore. It would have made more sense for her to leave by the front door. It's quicker to get to the King's Road that way too."

"Unless she didn't want to have to pass Gerald," said Dorothy almost to herself. "Do you think he could have overheard that Connie was going out via the garden?"

Mrs Platt looked confused. "It's possible, miss. He was up in the hall waiting for his taxi and I suppose my voice might carry."

Dorothy nodded. Like many people who were hard of hearing, Mrs Platt did indeed speak very loudly.

"Did he leave before or after Connie?" she asked.

Mrs Platt sighed and shook her head. "I don't know. You know what I'm like, miss. I didn't hear the door."

"And she never met you on the King's Road?"

"No even though she left here half an hour before we had arranged to meet. It sounds like she wanted to speak to me. Maybe she thought she'd meet me on my way from Fulham. I don't know. What do you think it all means, miss?" asked Jack.

"I'm not sure," she admitted and began walking towards the door. "I should be going, and I really don't think you should stay here, Jack."

"I need to know what happened to her. I'll go back as soon as I find out. I promise, miss."

Dorothy was struck by how young he seemed, but then

neither he nor Connie had yet turned twenty.

"He can't go home, miss. Just let him stay a while. He needs rest and a decent meal. Please don't say anything, miss," pleaded Mrs Platt.

"I understand and I won't say a word, but if I guessed he was here it's only a matter of time before someone else does."

She decided to walk from Chelsea back to Bloomsbury. It would take well over an hour but walking always helped her think and she needed to process everything she had learnt. If only Connie had told Mrs Platt why she was going to meet Jack early and what had made her act so strangely. Had she been killed shortly after she'd stepped out of the garden gate, or had she gone to Fulham, as Jack suggested, and been killed on her way back? But wouldn't she have gone to the King's Road to meet him instead? And where was Gerald? This investigation was getting more and more confusing. The inspector might have been able to make sense of it all, but she couldn't tell him what she'd discovered without betraying the trust of Mrs Platt and Jack.

"What a lovely evening to be out for a stroll, Miss Peto."

She looked up with a start. She'd been so deep in thought, she hadn't even noticed she was approaching Trafalgar Square, and strolling towards her was Eric Curtis. She nodded politely but didn't speak. She'd learnt her lesson and wasn't prepared to be drawn into a conversation with him again.

"You are wasting your time if you are looking for Gerry, Miss Peto. I can tell you he isn't at Ciro's."

Dorothy nodded again and continued on her way.

"I take it he hasn't showed up yet? Two of Derwent's

minions have already been asking after him. Perhaps all your time would be better spent making enquiries at the city morgues."

Dorothy couldn't help herself. She stopped and spun around. "You think he's dead?"

Eric shrugged. "That would be just Gerry's luck. About to inherit a fortune and he drops dead."

A thought suddenly struck her. "If he was dead, who would inherit then?"

Eric gave her a slow, lazy smile. He was toying with her again.

"Let me think. I imagine it would be his good lady wife—and a very deserving woman I hear she is too."

With that he raised his hat and sauntered away whistling.

Chapter Eighteen

"DOROTHY! DOROTHY!"

It was the following afternoon. Dorothy had been stuck in the office ploughing through enrolment forms all day and trying to decide what she should do about what Jack and Mrs Platt had told her. Not even regular visits from Margaret's dogs with their wet noses and wagging tails had cheered her up.

"Dorothy! Dorothy!"

Mary was calling her name, yet again, but Dorothy had decided to ignore her. She had been particularly demanding today. A second later, her cross face appeared around the door.

"Dorothy! Couldn't you hear me? I've been yelling my head off for you. There's a telephone call for you. It's Edith Smith and she's calling all the way from Grantham."

Dorothy quickly got to her feet and hurried through into the main office, mumbling an apology to Mary. She picked up the receiver and pressed it to her ear.

"Is that you, Edith?" she asked.

"Yes, Miss Peto. Can you hear me?"

"I can, just. Is something wrong?"

"I'm not sure but I'm a little concerned and I thought I

should speak with you. There's been a gentleman up here from London. He was at the nursing home asking about Jessica and I heard from the vicar that he had been to the church too. Asking questions and wanting to see the marriage register."

"Do you know his name?"

"No, but I caught a glimpse of him. He was in his thirties, I'd say. Tall with a thin face and fair hair that was too long for him to be in the army. I didn't like the look of him at all. I thought you should know."

"Thank you. Where is Jessica now? Is she still in Grantham?"

"Yes, but I don't know for how long. Someone at the hospital found out about her marriage and pregnancy. She has been asked to leave. I said she could stay with me, but after receiving your letter, I think she's considering coming to London."

Dorothy thought for a moment. From Edith's description, she was sure the man in Grantham was Gerald. If he had tracked Jessica down, it would be much safer for her to be in London. To her mind, he was still the main suspect for killing Hector and Connie.

"I think that would be a good idea. Ask her to send me a telegram with the details of the train she's taking and I'll meet her at King's Cross station."

As soon as she put the phone down on Edith, she picked it up again and asked to be put through to Inspector Derwent at Scotland Yard. After several minutes, she heard a voice at the end of the line, but it was Sergeant Clark not the inspector. She quickly repeated the information Edith had given her, but he didn't seem particularly perturbed.

"We've already circulated Gerald Gaskill's description, miss, and remember the inspector only wants to speak to him as a witness at this stage." She knew he was only trying to reassure her, but she did wish he would take her concerns more seriously.

"Please could you contact Chief Constable Casburn in Grantham and tell him Gerald could be there and that Jessica might be in danger?" she persisted.

There was a weary sigh at the other end of the line. "I'll see what I can do, miss," he replied.

Later that afternoon, a telegram arrived from Jessica. It said she would be arriving the next morning at ten o'clock. Dorothy carefully tucked it into her pocket. She would have preferred it if Jessica could have come to London that evening rather than spending another night in Grantham if Gerald was trying to find her, but there was really nothing more she could do.

WHEN SHE RETURNED to her flat that evening, she found letters from Nina and Raymond waiting for her on the doormat. She scooped them up and placed them on the hall table while she hung up her jacket, cringing a little at the thick layer of dust she had disturbed. She had been so busy recently that she had rather neglected her housekeeping chores, but the dusting would have to wait a little longer—she was desperate to hear the news from Nina and her brother.

She made a cup of tea, then curled up in the armchair to read both letters. Nina's was more like an adventure novel. There was a vivid description of her voyage and character sketches of many of her fellow travellers, then details of her arrival in Serbia. Dorothy thought her journey to the hospital on a donkey sounded rather terrifying and the lack of equipment on the wards must be desperate, but Nina's humour and indomitable spirit shone through in every line.

Raymond's letter was more sombre in tone. He told her about a letter he had received from Lady Sledmere, who was still grieving terribly. In response, he had sent her a letter, reassuring her that George's life may have been short, but it had been a happy one and that she had been a wonderful, loving mother. Both Dorothy and Raymond knew this wasn't quite true and that George had found both his parents rather cold and stern but, as Raymond wrote, 'did it really matter if it helped ease the pain of a grieving mother'? Dorothy carefully placed the letter back in its envelope. As she finished her tea, she recalled another conversation that had referred to a letter and a thought occurred to her.

It took her over an hour to locate Captain Boyle. He wasn't at any of the officers' clubs she could think of but she finally tracked him down at the Union Jack Club, the club for non-commissioned officers. She was thankful he was still in the capital and thought how typical it was that he should spend his free time with his men, before they all returned to the front. He sounded surprised to hear her voice.

"Miss Peto? How may I help you?"

"Captain Boyle, when I saw you in Southampton, you told me you had written to Lieutenant Gaskill's grandfather and wife. You told them he died instantly and didn't suffer. Was that really the truth?"

There was a pause at the end of the line. "My I ask why you should doubt my word, Miss Peto?"

"I'm sorry. I don't mean to, but I thought perhaps you wanted to protect them from the truth. It's terribly important. You see his grandfather was murdered on the same day Paul died."

"Really? At what time?"

"We believe at between ten o'clock on the Saturday evening and four o'clock on the Sunday morning. We all assumed Paul was killed in battle on the Saturday morning. However, if we can prove Paul died after, not before his grandfather, then it would make a huge difference to the lives of Jessica and her baby."

"Jessica is pregnant?"

"Yes."

There was another pause. "Very well then, Miss Peto. I'm afraid the contents of my letter to her and Paul's grandfather weren't entirely true. I wish they were. Paul did not die instantly. He was badly injured. That battle, well, it was the first time we had used poisonous gas. We wanted to give the Boche a taste of his own medicine, but it backfired. Literally. The gas was blown back on to our own men, including Paul. We managed to get him to a field hospital, but his lungs were ruined. He suffered terribly and died of his injuries."

"Do you know the exact time and date?" Hearing the catch in his voice, she hated to press him, but this was important.

"I do. I was with him at the end. It was ten o'clock on the Sunday morning. Twenty-four hours after we launched the attack."

"Please could you put that in a letter to Mr Arnold Pearson? He's the Gaskills' solicitor."

"Can you promise me you will do your utmost to ensure Jessica is never shown this letter or hears of its contents?"

"I promise."

"Very well then, Miss Peto. I shall."

"Thank you very much," she replied quietly but the line was already dead.

She put the telephone receiver down and let this news sink in. That poor young man was suffering in agony while she and Margaret had been standing in the garden staring down at the body of his grandfather. She shuddered at the thought of what he must have endured and vowed to do everything she could to protect Jessica from the truth, but now at least it seemed her future was secure. If what Mr Pearson had said about Hector dying intestate was true, then Paul would have inherited everything and now it would go to Jessica and her child. And Gerald wouldn't get a penny.

THE NEXT MORNING, Dorothy was running late. The clock at St Pancras Old Church was striking ten as she hurried by. Jessica's train would have arrived. It was all due to Mary and another of her stupid instructions. She'd insisted Dorothy stay and watch her demonstrate how to sew on the new WPS armbands to replace the WPV ones. As if Dorothy, or indeed any of the other women, weren't capable of sewing on an armband! A loud horn beeped at her as she was almost hit by an omnibus dashing across Euston Road and into King's Cross station.

The place was as busy as ever. She stopped a passing porter and asked him which platform Jessica would have arrived on and he directed her to the one farthest away. Dorothy began walking briskly to the footbridge when all of a sudden there was a shout and a scream. Dorothy ran towards the commotion. A woman had fallen down the bridge steps and was lying in a heap on the floor. As she got closer, she realised to her horror that it was Jessica. Quickly, she knelt down next to her and felt her pulse. She was alive but unconscious.

"Jessica! Jessica!" she repeated urgently while gently shaking her shoulder. She raised her head to look at the crowd of people around her. "Please, someone, send for an ambulance," she pleaded.

"Yes, miss," replied a young porter.

"Did anyone see what happened?" asked Dorothy.

"She missed her footing, fell and knocked her head," said an elderly man.

"No. She didn't fall. She was pushed," insisted the woman standing next to him. This statement was met with mutterings of agreement and disagreement in equal measure.

"Who pushed her?" asked Dorothy.

"I couldn't see him clearly. He was dressed in a long black overcoat and had his hat pulled down. I thought as soon as I saw him that this is no weather for a heavy overcoat, a trench coat maybe. I bet he was a foreigner. German no doubt."

This was greeted by yet more murmurs from the crowd.

"Did you see which way he went?" asked Dorothy.

"I'll go and tell the police to look out for the villain," offered the elderly gentleman.

"Please tell them to contact Inspector Derwent at Scotland Yard with the message that Jessica Gaskill has been attacked," said Dorothy.

"Of course, miss," he replied before shuffling off at a slower pace than Dorothy would have liked. No sooner was he out of sight, than the porter returned.

"An ambulance is on the way, miss," he reported, slightly out of breath. "Now come along, ladies and gentlemen, move along please. Nothing else to see here. Let the lady have some air."

Dorothy remained crouched on the floor holding Jessica's hand and cursing herself for being late to meet her. The ambulance arrived and the two stretcher-bearers carefully carried Jessica out of the station.

Dorothy travelled with Jessica in the ambulance, praying that the young woman and her baby would be safe, but she still hadn't regained consciousness. At the hospital, she was instructed to wait in the corridor while the doctors examined Jessica. It seemed to take forever. Over an hour later and there was still no word, then in the distance, she heard the sound of heaving footsteps echoing down the corridor accompanied by the tapping of a cane. A few seconds later, Inspector Derwent was by her side.

"How is she?" he asked raising his hat before taking the seat next to her.

"I don't know. She was still unconscious when we arrived. Nobody has told me anything. I'm trying to believe that no news is good news."

"That's true more often than you may think, Miss Peto."

"She was pushed by Gerald Gaskill, I'm sure of it. A woman at the station said she saw a man in a long overcoat and Edith Smith telephoned me to say a man had been in Grantham asking about Jessica. Did Sergeant Clark tell you? And I've discovered that Paul definitely died after Hector, so Jessica would be the beneficiary not Gerald. What if he had found that out too? It would be a reason to kill her. A motive."

Dorothy could hear how quickly she was talking and how strained her voice sounded, but she couldn't help it. It was always the same when she was emotional. She was desperate for the inspector to finally agree with her that Gerald was their man. He fixed his blue eyes on her, his face unreadable.

"That may well be the case, but Gerald did not push Jessica down the stairs." She opened her mouth to protest, but he held up his hand. "We fished his body out of the Thames this morning."

Chapter Nineteen

D OROTHY STARED AT him. Stunned into silence for a
second.

"He's dead?" she asked incredulously.

"Yes, he died last night, sometime after midnight according to Dr Stirk. We can't be sure if he fell, knocked his head and ended up in the river or if he was hit by someone, then thrown in."

Dorothy let his news sunk it. She'd been so sure Gerald had killed his uncle and probably Connie too. None of this made sense.

"But I thought he was in Grantham?" she finally replied.

"Perhaps he returned, or perhaps the man described to you wasn't Gerald."

"But it sounded like him. A man in his thirties, hair too long to be a soldier."

"Forgive me but that description could fit hundreds if not thousands of men and if I remember correctly from the photograph in the newspaper, Edith Smith wears glasses. She could have been mistaken."

"I don't understand it. I was convinced Gerald was responsible for everything. Who else could it be?"

"I've sent Taylor and Brook to pick up Duckworth

again. He at least had a motive for attacking Gerald, if he was indeed killed."

"If only you hadn't had to let him go again."

He ignored her barb. "And we are still trying to locate Jack Hurst."

She could feel her cheeks starting to burn.

"You haven't seen him, have you?"

"No. What makes you say that?"

"Your face has turned the colour of a ripe tomato."

Dorothy's hand automatically flew to her cheek and she quickly changed the subject. "You said you aren't sure if Gerald's death was an accident or murder."

"No."

"Has Willerby visited the scene too?" asked Dorothy. She valued the young scientist's opinion far more that the belligerent doctor's.

"He's there now. I'm going back to meet him when I leave here, but I wanted to see how Mrs Gaskill is. You are welcome to join me."

Dorothy was torn. She very much wanted to hear for herself what Willerby had to say but she didn't want to leave the hospital before she'd heard how Jessica was. Fortunately, she was saved from having to make a decision by the appearance of a matron in a well-starched uniform bustling towards them.

"Miss Peto, thank you for waiting," she said with a smile, then looking at the inspector. "Would you be Mr Gaskill?"

To Dorothy's amusement, the inspector turned slightly pink.

"No, Matron. This is Inspector Derwent of Scotland

Yard," she explained quickly, "How is Jessica?"

"I am happy to tell you both that Mrs Gaskill has regained consciousness. She is a little weak and confused still, but the doctor sees no reason why she won't make a full recovery."

"And the baby?" asked Dorothy.

"It is early days yet, Miss Peto, but the doctor says everything seems fine."

"May I see her?"

"I'm afraid not. She needs to rest. Perhaps you could return later this afternoon? Good day, both of you."

As she walked away, the inspector rose to his feet and offered Dorothy his hand.

"It seems there is nothing to keep you here, Miss Peto. Shall we?"

They arrived down at the river just as Gerald's body was being taken away. They both paused and bowed their heads as the stretcher went by before continuing to the water's edge. Dr Stirk had left but Willerby was there with Sergeant Clark and several uniformed officers.

"Good morning, Willerby. What's your opinion?" asked the inspector immediately.

"Good morning, Inspector, Miss Peto. I definitely believe he was attacked. Hit on the head with one of those loose bits of concrete from beneath the bridge," explained the scientist, gesturing to where the base of the bridge met the bank.

"Like Connie Beal. Have you found the piece of concrete?"

"No, and he had been in the water too long for there to

be any debris in the wound to his head, but there are dark stains on the grass just here. It's blood. I had a chance to look at the body too. The victim's necktie was missing, also a button from his evening coat."

"He was in evening dress?" interrupted Dorothy.

"Yes, Miss Peto," replied Willerby. "My theory is that Gerald's attacker hit him and rendered him unconscious. Then they used his necktie to attach something, possibly the piece of concrete that was used to hit him, to his ankle to weigh the body down, but it came loose and the body rose to the surface."

Dorothy was still confused by what he was wearing. If he had been in Grantham, then hurried back to London, where and when would he have changed? The police had been watching Cheyne Row and Emily's address. The inspector, however, was nodding his head.

"That's sounds plausible, Willerby. Did you discuss this theory with Dr Stirk? Did he concur?"

Willerby gave a rueful smile and shook his head.

"I did but he did not. The good doctor totally disagreed. 'A fanciful idea' was how he described it. He prefers the idea that Gerald was drunk and simply stumbled into the river. He thinks the results of the post-mortem examination will confirm his idea."

The inspector turned his attention to Sergeant Clark.

"Any word on Duckworth?"

"He has an alibi, sir," replied the sergeant. "He was drinking at his sister's pub from seven o'clock last night and by all accounts drank enough to sink a battleship. His sister and several other patrons reported that he passed out at around midnight. There was no way he could have got from Hackney to Chelsea let alone taken on Gerald Gaskill."

"What about Hurst?"

"No, sir. No sign of hide nor hair of him," replied Sergeant Clark.

"Let's pay twelve Cheyne Row another visit. Gaskill may have returned there with or without Mrs Platt hearing him. Willerby, why don't you join us? You may find something of interest in his bedroom. The missing button or necktie, perhaps."

The two detectives and Willerby started walking away, but Dorothy hung back. The inspector looked over his shoulder.

"Will you not be joining us, Miss Peto?"

Dorothy glanced in the direction of Cheyne Row. She had no idea if Jack was still there or not, but she wasn't sure she wanted to find out. The poor young man had seemed so desperately sad when she'd last seen him, she didn't think she could bear to watch him being taken into custody, knowing that he was either likely to face a court martial or be charged with murder by the inspector, who was rapidly running out of suspects.

"I think perhaps I'll return to the hospital," she said quietly. "I may be allowed to see Jessica. She might be able to say who pushed her."

The inspector raised an eyebrow, but simply inclined his head and said, "As you wish, Miss Peto. Good day."

When she returned to the hospital, Jessica was sleeping but the matron allowed Dorothy to sit by her bedside.

"Only five minutes, Miss Peto, and if she wakes up you

mustn't tire her out," she'd warned sternly.

After a few seconds, Jessica opened her eyes and smiled. "Hello, Dorothy. It's nice to see a friendly face."

"I'm so sorry I wasn't there to meet you at the station. I might have been able to stop whoever it was who pushed you."

"Nobody pushed me. I simply fell."

"Really?"

"Yes, it was my own fault. I've been feeling awfully tired and weak recently. Edith says it's understandable with all the worry and upset about Paul. I was holding on to the handrail as I came down the stairs and I looked up and saw a young man in uniform. Just for a second, I thought it was him, Paul. He was disappearing into the crowd. I wanted to go after him. I tried to hurry after him and I missed my footing." A tear rolled down her cheek. "Such a silly fool."

Dorothy reached out and squeezed her hand. "Not at all. The important thing is you are going to be all right. You and the baby."

Jessica sniffed and nodded. "The doctors say everything seems fine. The fall didn't harm him or her, thank heavens."

The matron appeared in the doorway, tapped the watch clipped to the front of her uniform and gave Dorothy a meaningful look.

"It looks like that is my cue to leave," Dorothy whispered. "I'll come and see you tomorrow and may I tell Emily Gaskill you are here? I know she will be concerned about you."

Jessica smiled. "She wrote me such a lovely letter. She even invited me to stay with her. I'm very lucky. You have both been so kind."

Dorothy kissed her goodbye and scuttled out of the ward before the formidable matron could scold her.

Once outside, she headed to the nearest post office and as promised, sent Emily a telegram, then hurried to catch the next tram to Bloomsbury. She arrived back at her flat feeling utterly exhausted. She sunk down on to the sofa without bothering to remove her hat or jacket. The sun was streaming in through the window and showed just how grubby the place was looking. Every surface needed a good dust and the windows themselves could do with a wash. Her eyes settled on the gilt mirror above the fireplace. That was in need of a good polish too. It would take a whole day to get the place looking shipshape again.

Then suddenly as she stared at her reflection, all those thoughts that had been swirling around in her mind for days fell into place. She dashed back to the front door and out into the city.

Chapter Twenty

S HE COULD HEAR the music from Ciro's as soon as she turned on to Orange Street. The doorman looked her up and down and shook his head.

"Members only, miss."

"If you would rather, I can call Inspector Derwent of Scotland Yard. I'm sure he could be here with several uniformed officers in a matter of minutes, but neither of us want to cause your customers any alarm."

He glared at her for a moment, then to her relief he stepped aside.

"Go on then if you must, but don't go stirring up any trouble."

Dorothy hurried through the door before he changed his mind, then paused for a second to allow her eyes to adjust to the dimness. The place was heaving. The dance floor was packed with couples swaying as the band played 'They Didn't Believe Me' and Dorothy, was immediately reminded of Raymond and George.

There was no sign of Eric Curtis, but through the cigarette smoke, she spotted Bessie, sipping a cocktail at the bar. Dressed in amethyst satin with long matching gloves and still wearing her dark glasses.

"He's let you out on your own, has he?" she said when Dorothy got closer. "You come to ask me more questions?"

"I'm not here to talk to you as a representative of the police, but as a woman."

Bessie barked out a laugh. "What do you know about being a woman like me? You and me are from different worlds. You don't know anything about me."

"I know you used to work as Hector Gaskill's parlour maid before Ruth Platt. I know Gerald seduced you and Hector dismissed you and you ended up here."

"How do you know? Did Mrs Platt say something? Or that old drunk Duckworth?"

"No. One of Mr Gaskill's neighbours said that two parlour maids had been dismissed and the first time I met you, you made a comment about how to make the mirrors shine," explained Dorothy pointing to the mirror behind the bar. Bessie smiled and shook her head.

"I was a good maid. I worked hard. When old Mr Gaskill caught me and Gerald, he dismissed me without references. Do you know how hard it is to get a respectable job without references? It was do this or starve. Gerald found me a place here."

Dorothy lowered her voice. "Was it him who gave you syphilis?"

Bessie flinched. "How dare you!" she hissed. "I'll not stay here and be insulted by the likes of you."

With that she jumped down from her bar stool, snatched up her gloves and parasol and stomped across the dance floor, pushing couples out of her way and out through the door. Dorothy chased after her, but the dancers didn't move out of her way so readily and when she got out into the street, Bessie was nowhere to be seen. She turned to the doorman.

"Where did she go?"

"Where did who go?" he replied with a smirk. Dorothy decided to act on an idea she'd had since the day they'd found the smashed watch and headed towards the river. Halfway down Northumberland Avenue she saw her. With her vivid purple dress and parasol, she was easy to spot. Dorothy broke into a run and caught up with her as she crossed the Strand. Behind her moored on the river was the barge, the *Lady Elizabeth*. Bessie spun around at the sound of her running feet.

"You followed me," she said sounding more surprised than angry.

"Yes, although I thought you might come here to the river. I thought I saw you one day, and Eric described you as a drifter, but I didn't understand what he meant at first."

"I've always said he talks too much. You'd better come aboard now you are here."

Bessie stepped onto the barge with one easy fluid movement and Dorothy did the same although a little more clumsily. Bessie gestured for her to take a seat on the curved bench at the helm, while she unlocked the little wooden door and ducked inside. She returned a moment later with two glasses and a stoneware bottle and poured a couple of fingers of clear liquid into each glass. She handed one to Dorothy and silently toasted her before taking a drink. Dorothy sniffed cautiously. It was gin. She took a sip and tried not to grimace. She rarely drank except for the occasional glass of champagne. Bessie's lips curved into a small smile. The sun was beginning to set, but she didn't remove her glasses.

"I'm sorry if I offended you. I know you're trying to hide your condition. That's why you wear those glasses. Your eyes have been affected."

Bessie's smile disappeared. "An occupational hazard, some call it," she replied. "It wasn't Gerald who gave it to me. I don't know who did. It could have been any of them, but it was his fault I was there. I was just a child. I didn't stand a cat in hell's chance. He said he'd take care of me. Like a fool, I believed him."

"Is that why you killed him?"

Bessie's face remained impassive. She merely exhaled slowly. "It was just one reason on a very long list. He'd destroyed enough lives. Mine, Ruth's, Emily's and he ended Hector's and Connie's."

"He admitted killing his uncle?"

"He had to. He needed me to give him an alibi."

"Why did you help him?"

"Money. I can't work anymore. Eric lets me drink in the club, but nothing else. Soon he probably won't even let me do that. Gerald said if I told the police we were together all night he would pay up as soon as he inherited. It was partly true, what I said. We were together all night, but just not the way you thought. He wouldn't touch me in case I passed it on to him."

"Instead, you came down here to your barge and went down the river to Chelsea."

"Murdo Channing is an uncle of mine. We moored up a little way along from him and his family. Gerald had already killed Hector before he left and he destroyed the will. He knew as soon as he signed that he'd been written out and that the old skinflint wouldn't have paid for two, but he didn't bargain on him being so tight-fisted he'd got his solicitor to reuse parts of the original will." She grinned and topped up both glasses although Dorothy had barely touched hers. "He hit him with a candlestick and left him propped up in his chair. He knew Connie and Mrs Platt had gone to bed. He made sure Duckworth caught a glimpse of Hector in his chair and told him not to disturb him. Then gave him a decanter of brandy to drink himself into a stupor."

"So you arrived in Chelsea a little before half past three. Gerald went back to the house and unlocked the library door with the key he'd already taken, dragged his uncle's body outside and tried to make it look like he'd fallen and banged his head when he'd gone to feed the birds. Then returned to you on the barge and dropped the candlestick in the river and spent the rest of the night there with you."

"Nobody was going to look for him on the river. I went to bed, and he sat up in the galley smoking until the early hours."

"With the door open?"

Bessie nodded.

"Did Murdo see him?"

"It didn't matter if he did or not. If he was with me, Murdo wouldn't say anything."

"You didn't feel guilty at all about Hector?"

"No. Why should I? I'm an expert on cruel and cold men and he was one of the worst."

"What about Connie? Was she blackmailing Gerald?"

Bessie shook her head. "No, but she'd worked out he had killed his uncle. Gerald didn't know how but said he saw it in her face."

"I think it was the whistling," explained Dorothy. "She'd heard someone whistling just before she found Hector's body and Mrs Platt said Connie froze when she saw Gerald come down the stairs whistling."

"That could have been it," agreed Bessie. "Gerald always whistled when he smoked. Anyway, he guessed she was going to run off to tell her young man, so he went out the front door and round the back to catch up with her. He thought he was being clever offering her money to keep quiet. He turned on the charm and told her that once he'd inherited, he'd be able to provide for Mrs Platt, Ruth and her baby. He's the father in case you hadn't realised. Poor Ruth. I was planning to give them some of his dirty money too."

Dorothy nodded as Bessie continued.

"At first Connie agreed. She took the money he offered. I think she was just trying to get away from him and Gerald must have thought the same. He hit her as she turned to go, then hit her again. She begged him not to. Tried to appeal to his better nature. If she'd come to me, I'd have told her Gerald didn't have a better nature."

She gave a sharp laugh and started coughing. She took a handkerchief and dabbed at her mouth, removing some of her thick makeup and revealing the sores beneath.

"'I shut the little tart up.' That's what he said to me when he arrived at Ciro's, like he was proud of it. What's more, he wanted to kill again. He wanted to kill the girl Paul had married. He was here last night talking to me about it."

She took another drink. "It seems he found out about her when he read Emily's letter at his flat. He sometimes went there when he knew she would be out. Anyway, he got it into his head that this Jessica person might get in the way of him getting his hands on Hector's money. Last night, he came straight here from the station. He thought he was so clever hiding from the police. He was telling me all about how he'd been up north to try to find Paul's widow while he was changing into the evening clothes he'd left here. The same clothes he'd worn when he killed Connie. That's when I knew I had to stop him. I persuaded him to stay here for a drink. I said it was too risky going out to Ciro's or anywhere else. He agreed, took off his jacket, put his feet up and made himself comfortable. When he wasn't looking, I pulled off a button, then made a big show of noticing it. I put the idea in his head that it might have come off when he killed Connie. He started to panic and I offered to go down to Chelsea and help him look for it. It was the middle of the night. Nobody was there. We stepped out on to the embankment. Then when he knelt down, I picked up a piece of concrete from near the bridge and smashed him over his head as hard as I could. Then I used his necktie and tied the concrete to his ankle and rolled him into the river." She took another drink of gin. "I stood in the moonlight and watched him sink and wished I'd done it years ago."

Then she threw the rest of the gin down her throat. "Arrest me. Do what you want. What does it matter? I'll be dead before long."

"I couldn't arrest you even if I wanted to. It's not in my power." Dorothy took a card out of her pocket and handed it to her. "This is the address of the Lock Hospital. You should go there. They can help. There's a treatment now."

Bessie shook her head violently.

"No fear. I've heard about the treatment. They'll give me arsenic. They'll poison me."

"You are already being poisoned. If you don't get treatment soon, you'll go blind and those dark glasses of yours won't be able to hide that." She reached out and took hold of Bessie's gloved hand. "You have been so brave. Don't give in. Keep fighting."

They sat in silence for a few moments watching the river and listening to the water lap against the barge. Then Dorothy stood up and stepped on to the shore.

"Thank you, Bessie. Goodnight."

It was late when she returned home, and she was so exhausted she only just manged to undress herself before falling on to her bed and into a deep sleep.

The next morning, she went straight to Scotland Yard. On the way there, she practised everything she wanted to say to Inspector Derwent in her head. As she walked through the door she almost bumped into Mary and Margaret.

"Dorothy, what are you doing here?" demanded Mary immediately.

"I'm here to see Inspector Derwent."

"How strange—we are here to see Sir Edward Henry," began Margaret. "In fact, I think we may soon have some rather good news…"

But Dorothy wasn't listening. "I'm sorry, Margaret, you will have to tell me about it later. I'm in rather a rush."

"You are in danger of becoming as rude as Nina!" Mary

called after her.

Dorothy found Inspector Derwent in the incident room but he wasn't alone. Mr Pearson was with him, looking as flustered as ever.

"Good morning, Miss Peto," he said brightly. "I won't keep the inspector a moment if you wish to speak to him. I'm merely trying to establish when Hector and Gerald's bodies may be released. Emily is anxious they should be laid to rest."

"Of course," replied Dorothy. "Actually, I'm pleased to see you, Mr Pearson. I telephoned Captain Boyle recently and he confirmed that Paul did not die until ten o'clock on the morning we discovered his grandfather's body, so after Hector by several hours. He will be writing to you with all the details, although he and I would both rather Jessica didn't find out about how Paul died, especially in her condition."

The solicitor started mopping his brow with his spotted handkerchief. "No, no of course not. Well goodness me. This changes everything. I should contact Dennis and discover if this letter has arrived."

"You are welcome to use the telephone in my office, Mr Pearson," offered Inspector Derwent.

"Thank you, Inspector. Please excuse me, Miss Peto."

"What made you think to call Captain Boyle?" asked the inspector as soon as they were alone.

"Something my brother wrote in a letter to me. He said how in some circumstances, it is better to be kind than completely honest."

"I see."

Dorothy cleared her throat and began the speech she had been preparing, hoping to make it sound as natural as possible.

"I haven't just spoken to Captain Boyle. I've also been to see Bessie Shelton. I wanted to ask her about Gerald. She told me he was with her before he died. He'd had a few drinks and admitted killing his uncle and Connie. While he was with her, he discovered he was missing a button from his jacket. He was worried that it might have come off when he killed Connie, so he went back to look for it."

The inspector raised an eyebrow and surveyed her silently for a moment. "I suppose she told you that he wasn't wearing his necktie when he left her too."

"Yes, she did as a matter of fact."

"So it could be possible that he simply slipped, knocked his head and fell into the river."

"Well Doctor Stirk thought so, and he did think Gerald had been drinking heavily."

"Which he confirmed after the post-mortem, late yesterday afternoon. Enough to sink a battleship to use one of Sergeant Clark's favourite expressions."

"Is that the end of the matter? You won't be investigating Gerald's death any further? Or charging Bessie with withholding evidence or anything like that?"

"Not if she is willing to make a statement regarding Gerald admitting to being Hector and Connie's killer."

"Oh I'm sure she will, but perhaps it could wait until she has started her treatment. I've advised her to go to the Lock Hospital. She's suffering from syphilis, you see. Hence the dark glasses."

"Not just a silly affectation?"

"No."

"I do hope you will be receiving more letters from your brother in the future. They seem to cause quite the chain reaction."

Dorothy could feel the colour rising to her cheeks. "Is there any news of Jack Hurst?" she asked quickly. She'd been wondering if they had found him. To her surprise, it was the inspector's turn to look uncomfortable.

"Strangely, it seems he'd been in the custody of the Metropolitan police all along."

"Is that so?" she asked in surprise.

"He'd been arrested for being drunk and disorderly while on leave and was being held at Fulham police station. When they heard we were looking for him, they handed him over to us and we held him for questioning in regard to the death of Gerald Gaskill. I explained the situation to his commanding officer and apologised for any confusion. It was merely a lack of communication between stations. Jack won't face any charges from either ourselves or the military police."

He relayed all this without once looking her in the eye. It seemed he did have a kind heart after all and was just as good at twisting a story to suit his own needs as she was. She was sorely tempted to tease him a little but at that moment, Mr Pearson returned not looking any calmer than when he'd left.

"Dennis confirmed that a letter arrived from Captain Boyle in the first post. He read it out to me, and it is just as you said, Miss Peto. Poor, poor Paul. How he must have suffered," he said, shaking his head sadly.

"But what does it mean for Jessica and her unborn child? Will she be entitled to any of Mr Gaskill's estate?" asked Dorothy thinking of the pregnant young widow who was all alone in the world.

"All of it," replied the solicitor sounding unusually confident. "As I explained when we first met, Miss Peto, if an individual dies without a valid will, then the rules of intestate apply. The closest living relative gets everything. We now know that in Hector's case this was Paul and he in turn left everything to his wife. I shall visit the new Mrs Gaskill and explain everything. I'm sure you'll both be pleased to know she was discharged from hospital this morning."

"She was? Where is she now?" asked Dorothy in surprise.

"She's tucked up at twelve Cheyne Row, which is rather apt as it's her house now."

"Surely she isn't there all alone?" enquired Dorothy.

"No, no. Emily is there. She went to the hospital yesterday evening, when she received your telegram and it was her idea that Jessica should convalesce at Cheyne Row. She thought it would be what Paul would have wanted. Mrs Platt is taking good care of the invalid too. She's already making nutritious soups and supplying endless cups of strong sweet tea, I understand."

Dorothy smiled. She could just imagine the cook enjoying having someone to fuss over. Mr Pearson chattered on.

"I also believe Mrs Platt's niece and great-nephew will be joining them. Emily had always been aware of their situation and she was keen to see the family united under one roof. Mrs Platt will continue to cook, and her niece will act as maid. Emily is going to help find a nursemaid or mother's help, or whatever they are called to assist Jessica at the appropriate time too. Although I dare say when the baby arrives, it will be hard to keep dear Emily away."

"What about poor Emily?" asked Dorothy. "She rather seems to have lost out in all of this."

The solicitor's face flushed bright red as he cleared his throat. "I hope I may have been able to remedy that situation, Miss Peto. Last night, Emily did me the great honour of accepting the offer of my hand in marriage. Naturally, we shall have to wait a proper amount of time to pass before making an official announcement, but I couldn't not tell you two dear people."

"What wonderful news!" exclaimed Dorothy. "I am so pleased for you both."

The solicitor looked like he might start a jig he was so happy. Inspector Derwent reached out and shook his head. "Yes, congratulations, Pearson."

"Thank you. Thank you. Now if you will excuse me, I must dash. As wonderful as it is that Jessica has entered our lives, the happy event has generated rather a lot of paperwork. Good day."

Dorothy and the inspector stood side by side in silence and watched the solicitor hurry away. They winced in unison as he only narrowly missed bumping into a tea trolley as he dashed down the corridor.

"What a lovely man Mr Pearson is. I think he and Emily will be very happy together. If I ever have need of a solicitor, I shall be certain to call on him."

"Really?" asked the inspector.

"Why the note of surprise in your voice? Don't you like him?"

"Like doesn't come into it, Miss Peto. I simply don't consider him to be a particularly competent lawyer. I can't help thinking that if he had kept a copy of Hector Gaskill's will, we could all have been saved an awful lot of trouble. Mr Gaskill might even still be alive."

"That's a little harsh. And besides it sounds as if everything has turned out rather well, all things considered."

"Perhaps a little like Miss Boyle being ousted from the Women Police Volunteers."

"She wasn't ousted, at least not exactly, she resigned. Hold on, what does Nina have to do with anything?"

The corner of his mouth curled up just a little. "I was merely drawing a comparison between the two events. The deaths of Hector and Paul Gaskill, and Connie, although tragic, led to Mrs Platt and her niece having a more secure future and Emily a far happier life. Miss Boyle resigning led you to expressing a wish to leave the WPV, which in turn led to Miss Damer Dawson accepting my formal request for your assistance here at Scotland Yard."

"You have requested a transfer for me!" she exclaimed in delight. "Really? I will be working with you and the other detectives?"

"As Sergeant Clark pointed out, we see rather a lot of you anyway. It seemed sensible to make the arrangement official."

"Gosh! I don't know what to say. If you hadn't just become my superior officer, I think I might embrace you."

"I would be inclined to discourage embracing anyone superior or otherwise while on duty. I have always found a firm handshake or in extreme circumstances an encouraging slap on the back to be more than adequate."

"When do I start?"

"Assuming you don't stumble across any dead bodies in the next twenty-four hours, I shall see you tomorrow morning, Miss Peto. Now I shall wish you a good day. I need to find Brook and Taylor and update them on recent events." Then, taking her completely by surprise, he reached out and gave her hand a firm shake. "Welcome aboard, Miss Peto." Then with a tip of his hat, he was gone.

Dorothy allowed herself a moment alone to enjoy the feeling of being in the incident room, knowing it would soon be her place of work, before hurrying back downstairs to find Margaret and thank her. Then she should write to tell Nina her news immediately. Her friend would be thrilled for her. Finally, she was on her way to becoming a proper policewoman.

THE END

Author's Note

A Death in Chelsea is a work of fiction inspired by real people and real events. Dorothy Peto, Nina Boyle, Mary Allen and Margaret Damer Dawson were all founding members of the Women Police Volunteers.

My character, Dorothy, is a combination of several suffragettes and pioneering policewomen. The real Dorothy spent much of the First World War in Bristol and Bath, only visiting London occasionally for training.

A disagreement over the Defence of the Realm Act really did lead to Nina resigning as deputy commandant of the WPV, although she didn't leave to become a nurse in Serbia until 1916. Mary did take over Nina's role and, in agreement with Margaret, changed the name of the organisation to the Women's Police Service.

Edith Smith was the first woman to be attested, although the ceremony actually took place on the 17th December 1915. In 2014, following a campaign by local police officers in Grantham, Theresa May, the then Home Secretary, unveiled a plaque in her memory.

Although there is no record of Dorothy ever visiting Edith in Grantham, the two women did spend three weeks patrolling the parks of London together. In her memoirs, Dorothy describes Edith as 'a woman of outstanding personality, fearless, motherly and adaptable'.

Acknowledgements

I hope you enjoyed this second Lady in Blue Mystery and that perhaps you will want to discover more about Dorothy, Edith, Nina, Mary, Margaret and the work of the Women's Police Service. I am very grateful to the following authors whose books helped me research the story of Dorothy and her companions or provided background for this period in our history.

Allen, Mary Sophia, *Lady in Blue: Reminiscences and Study of the Status of Women Police*, S. Paul, 1936

Frances, Hilary, *The Sexual Politics of Four Edwardian Feminists from c.1910 to c.1935*, etheses.whiterose.ac.uk, 1996

Lock, Joan, *The British Policewoman: Her Story*, Robert Hale Ltd, 1979

Peto, Miss Dorothy Olivia Georgiana OBE, *The Memoirs of*, Organising Committee for the European Conference on Equal Opportunities in the Police, 1992

White, Jerry, *Zeppelin Nights: London in the First World War*, Vintage, 2015

There are also several organisations I should like to thank for their invaluable assistance.

Black Country Living Museum
Grantham Civic Society
Greater Manchester Police Museum and Archives
National Archives
Police Firearms Officers Association
West Midlands Police Museum
University of York, Centre for Women's Studies

The Lady in Blue Mystery series

Book 1: *The Body in Seven Dials*

Book 2: *A Death in Chelsea*
View the series here!

Book 3: *The Mystery of the Missing Frenchman*

Available now at your favorite online retailer!

More Books by H L Marsay

The Chief Inspector Shadow series

Book 1: *A Long Shadow*

Book 2: *A Viking's Shadow*

Book 3: *A Ghostly Shadow*

Book 4: *A Roman Shadow*

Book 5: *A Forgotten Shadow*

Book 6: *A Christmas Shadow*

Book 7: *A Stolen Shadow*

The Secrets of Hartwell series

Book 1: *Four Hidden Treasures*

Book 2: *Four Secrets Kept*

Book 3: *Four Silences Broken*

Available now at your favorite online retailer!

About the Author

H L Marsay always loved detective stories and promised herself that one day, she would write one too. She is lucky enough to live in York, a city full of history and mystery. When not writing, the five men in her life keep her busy – two sons, two dogs and one husband.

Thank you for reading

A Death in Chelsea

If you enjoyed this book, you can find more from all our great authors at TulePublishing.com, or from your favorite online retailer.

TULE
PUBLISHING

Printed in Great Britain
by Amazon

51299175R00148